Houses from Another Street

A NOVEL

Michael Thurston

Copyright © 2019 Michael Thurston
All rights reserved
Printed in the United States of America

Printed and bound by
Levellers Press 2019 • Amherst, Massachusetts

ISBN 978-1-945473-85-2

"... an interrupted cry
Came over houses from another street,

But not to call me back or say good-bye."

Robert Frost, "Acquainted with the Night"

I

I.

BEFORE THE WORK, THE RITUALS. *He should loosen up about these. He has been urged, in fact, by professors and fellow students, by, of course, parents as well, though they are, happily, far away, rarely to be confronted aside from the upcoming Family Weekend (a dreaded dark spot on the calendar hanging to one side of the window), has been urged to try, just try, starting in on his homework without first aligning pencils just so, just so the pad of paper, too, and the notebook open to the passage he's supposed to revise. An opening assignment from Dr. Seymour: "Write about what brought you here." Intentionally open-ended, she said during the first tutorial. He tends to ruminate, he has been told. His rituals are not, by the way, problems at all, but pleasures, really, ways of taking appropriately slow, deliberate pleasure in such pleasing things as this prospect—as he opens the window exactly four inches— of the courtyard, autumn leaves aflame in the early evening light, the whole contained and given significant shape by the clean, white window frame. There is German homework, too, which he enjoys and might use to put off the revision for which he is not yet in the mood, though there, too, he can't allow himself to go on until he has gotten the fourth word right. Red blossoms against the white of snow, he sees, again, on the page to which he has opened the notebook. What brought him here. The poetic paradox of the image, one that sticks in the mind, that compels him to explore, to study, to locate its origins in a variety of historical, cultural, literary, and spiritual traditions. He has, as usual, secreted half an oatmeal cookie in the pocket of his tweed jacket. Jackets no longer required at dinner but why be at such a storied institution if not to be in its traditions as well as its spaces, the dressing for dinner as crucial an aspect of the place as its long* wood-floored corridors, its dark-paneled library of leather-bound wisdom. One works hard to arrive at such a place, and he will live and work and dress here just as had those generations who built the walls, the halls, the windows, and the wisdom. He has the cookie, not, strictly, legally (all food by rule to stay in the refectory), but the occasional mild infraction is, he supposes, as traditional as anything at such a place, and anyway, it is not for himself. He is as disciplined about snacking as about studying. It is, now, the cookie, crumbs and fragments, scattered along the brick just outside the open window, an evening treat for his regular guest, Gabriel, the least skittish and most social of the colony of squirrels for whom the courtyard trees are an autumn buffet.

Least skittish is one way to describe good old Gabe, but in fact the squirrel is a bully, bigger than the others, sleek with nut fat and shortening, lording it over the chittering underclass of skinny squirrels, the ones digging and delving in the leaves, around the roots, building and burying the winter stores that the survivors, those not squashed by cars or shrunken in gutters, will later subsist on. It may be that, in his unwitnessed hours, Gabriel does his bit, shelling and storing, but, what with all the cookie crumbs and, no doubt, muscling his way into any other squirrel's cache, it seems unlikely. There may linger, beneath his gray fur and his bulk, the cowardice conventionally assumed in bullies, but, after some initial wariness, the squirrel is almost casual, almost relaxed now as he steps from limb to lintel and nibbles at a cookie. The trick is to ignore him, or pretend to, stare at the pages of a book open on the desk, to sit, poised, pen in hand, to scribble, even, every now and then, a note in the margin or a line on the pad, keeping him in the periphery. Soon enough, the squirrel is going to become complacent, to take bits of nut or cookie from his hand, and that's when he is going to strangle it.

Soon, but not tonight. He's got to get a start on this assignment. "Write about what brought you here."

2.

THE FIRST TIME I SPIED ON NICOLE ROSE WAS AN ACCIDENT. Late night, door creak, the haven of shadow beneath the mimosa in her yard.

I had been long acquainted with the neighborhood by sodium streetlight, was more at ease in the dark than by daylight for reasons not vampirical but practical. Here (Centertown, Texas) there was no place that did not see you; you must dine late, then wander. A creaking front door, a quiet groan loud in the larger quiet of the night, me jumpy already anyway, Toms rampaging as they were, me wary of what might be waiting or coming up behind, all these bid me slide into the deeper dark and sidle upside the trunk, sharing with the opener and closer of the door at least the wish to keep things quiet, the screen closing with a careful click. The substance in the shadows sat, the porch just steps from where I stood (wishing I had chosen a better hiding place) and then there was a *snick-snick* and the lighter caught and in the flame Nicole Rose was illuminated as she lit a cigarette. It was dark again, then, the silhouette on the stoop still except for when the dimly glowing ember moved and, when she raised it to her lips and drew, brightened.

I believed in many things that fall of 1979: the statements of the Nicene Creed, the exceptional virtue of the United States of America, the advice my track coach and the abuse my father dispensed, and, vaguely, that two people who had never exchanged words aloud might communicate some subtle wordless thing to one another as they occupied the same space at the right time, questions of light and shadow, pulse, panic, and passion all certainly to be considered. Just as the smoke rose from Nicole's lips and dispersed and dissipated in the humid night, soon to become a scented whisper of the air I breathed, some aspect of spirit might emanate, waft, mingle, and an understanding form somewhere in the dark beneath the level of consciousness, beneath the shadows of the porch and the mimosa.

Breezeless and warm, late September still late summer, the night was disturbed, here, at least, on Nicole's street, only by the hum of air conditioners, the racket of my heart, riotous as the Payne High marching band. Nicole Rose: sixteen going on twenty, a worldly woman already, makeup-masked and armored day and evening in leather and denim, silent when not smoking with Heidi D'Amico after school, protected from even a too-long glance by her *hermano*, Hector, whose Camaro lurked now, dormant, dangerous, against the curb. A woman in the world I lived in only accidentally. Supernatural, untouched except by the dropouts she dated, friends of her brother, fellows of the same fraternity ("Dupree Body / No Muff Too Tuff"), untouchable by any force that through the corridors of Payne drove freshmen like me. I tasted her distant breath, tinct with Turkish and domestic tobaccos, and held my own, knowing that to be caught here was to lose more even than the night had cost me already, my balls the newest ornament to hang from the rearview of Hector Rose's muscle car, so I was still when she stood, though I could have stroked, as she passed, her hair that I had never before seen released from its restraints and let down past her shoulders, could have touched the baseball-sleeved T on whose front I could see, when she stood in the puddle of orange light the streetlight cast, number one, the cover of *Greetings from Asbury Park* reproduced and, number two, that no bra or other garment encumbered, beneath that flimsy cotton blend, her breasts. The cigarette, when she expertly flicked it, traced a sparking arc toward the storm drain.

There she stood, then, ankle deep in the orange pool, bare feet on the cracked pavement, between me and a retreat through the park and back to my own block. Gazing up, it seemed, into the vaulted dark beyond the streetlight, Nicole gently pressed her palms against her breasts, massaging herself for a long moment, stroking with her thumbs as she lifted, and the pleasure in this was audible in her long sigh. What I knew of desire could fit into the palm of my own hand, whether it held the tattered pages of a coverless *Playboy* Fats Crandall and I had kept in our fort in the woods or, frequently, the key to Onan's kingdom, and my palms tingled then to touch with hers the unimaginable textures of T-shirt and tenderness.

The moment over, she returned—careful creak of door and click of latch, the chunking of the lock's tongue into place, traces, still, of her smoke in the breezeless breath of the night. I had been often up and down these streets, had been out again and back again from my house through the neighborhoods of this, the southern, older part of Centertown. I had been well beyond them, too, had roamed from the munitions plant all the way out to the new subdivisions on the north side, the former pasturelands succumbing, half-acre by half-acre, to landscaped lots and pastiche palaces, could figure on the fly a dozen ways from any A to any B not from an explicit effort to chart Centertown but just because I had crisscrossed the town so many times. You could go anywhere at night, you could see without being seen, it was safer than anything done by daylight.

Usually.

My forays were not typically on foot, and had I been, as usual, mounted up and moving swiftly through the side streets, I'd have missed that moment under the mimosa, Nicole Rose beneath the streetlight, but my bike was, at that point, a bent disaster, a broken corpse stuck between junipers and wooden fence behind the bank, its spokes and spine victims of a thousand pounds of Payne Pirates' offensive line, the Toms. I would rebuild it, make it better, stronger, faster than it used to be, but that was for the next day and the six million weeks' worth of allowance it might cost, and when on unfamiliar foot I felt my way back home and slipped inside and plugged my headphones in and set the needle down on *Greetings from Asbury Park,* Nicole stood still in the orange light and her eyes found me in the dark as her thumbs stroked the soft skin swelling there beneath the cotton, and as we lay together in the lava-lit night, she was my Mary, Queen of Arkansas.

Centertown by sunlight: an unfocused suburb blurring into its neighbors, just another indistinct bead on the necklace strung from Dallas to Fort Worth. Unplanned, like many of us, growing up in asphalt, concrete, brick, and mulch from south to north, branching from Payne Firearms and a failed pipeline project over tamed tributaries of the Trinity. Payne High was indistinguishable from the industrial parks clotting the arteries of the Metroplex, another low building, dun and windowless in its apron of parking lots and acreage of athletic fields, a manor at the center of its tilth. At the back, a diamond modestly glowed and beside it bleachers rose along the stadium's straightaways, the eight-lane cinder track staying out of the way, yielding, like we all did, to the centrality of football, for which the lovingly maintained emerald at the brilliantly lit rectangular heart of the stadium was reserved. Not a Permian Basin powerhouse or regular contender for the championship, the Centertown team received nevertheless homage and obeisance from the rabble. They were legends in the corridors, deferred to and applauded as much by teachers as by their cowed cohorts, none more so than the Toms, a set of specially bred Spartans reared to work together as the O-line and enable the predictable three-yard between-the-tackles smash-mouth four-down style that had, since the fifties, been the team's trademark. With what reverence they were spoken of, praised even for their pummeling of those innocents we periodically sacrificed to them, imitated for the flat-tops, much to the pleasure and profit of their shared barber, Raider, taciturn bombardier deafened during missions over Dresden, our barber, too, though his look of something like disgust during my monthly five minutes in the chair made clear that, where he shaved the back and sides of the Toms for love, he was trimming me for money.

Among the Toms' adorers was my father, a former tackle himself, analyst and respecter of line play during his Friday nights in the stands. That, he said, was real work, real smarts, though it happened where nobody saw it, in the x's and o's, the schemes and twists and pulls and stunts and sweeps, god-damn did you see the way Tom cross-blocked to get that first down. Giants and geniuses, those Toms, what smarts did it take, after all, to run around in circles. Oval, I said. The track is an oval. Giants and geniuses and nobody with any sense would cross their paths. You stayed close to the walls as the Toms came crashing down the corridors of Payne, stayed off the streets post-game on Friday nights when, win or lose, they tore around town in one Tom's Duster, muscled up and mufflered to a unique rumble when idling, a gut-dumping roar when revved, jumping out to whale on any kid the fates offered up. Anyone with an ounce of sense stayed in, but as my father would tell anyone who stood still long enough, I had no sense, what sense did you need to run around in circles? Oh, excuse me. Ovals?

But the streets of Centertown by night, that was where I lived. Certain cyclist suicide by day, they were gorgeous slalom courses after hours. You could pick up speed on the downhill of Pipeline Road and zigzag the lanes, swoop in tight waves through the raised reflectors, detour through a drive-through lane. The parking lot of the new Target, unbroken asphalt acres across from the somber Lowry Funeral Home, beckoned and I spent nights sprinting the perimeter, zipping at top speed through the steel-bar chutes where shoppers were supposed to leave their carts. The history of Centertown was rehearsed every year in school pageants and any kid could tell you of the hearty German pioneers who had built near this unnamed branch of the Trinity, how from a cluster of farms and a general store the town had sprung to modern life, thanks to defense manufacturers and oilmen, how the new highway connecting Dallas and Fort Worth had transformed Centertown into a place to sleep and mow the lawn between commutes. But it was something else, something no other kid knew, to map the town's lifespan with the wheels of a ten-speed, to feel the broken pavements and weedy yards of neighborhoods like mine, the oldest that branched out from the highway by the plant, smooth, on the other side of Pipeline, to the newer cul-de-sacs around the midtown shopping centers, and bloom, beyond the high school, in the new subdivisions, two-story houses with taller trees in larger yards. And you could see the present just as powerfully as you could feel the past, the town transformed by darkness, quieted and calmed, relaxed as the man rocking his baby to sleep in an old steel lawn chair on Bel-Aire Drive, as the topless woman brushing her hair, oblivious alike to the bobbing of her breasts and the weight of my stare, as the couple having furtive, half-clothed sex on the loading dock of Mott's department store. You could see without being seen.

Unless, distracted by the spectacle of sex in the nest of broken-down cardboard, by shadows writhing in the shadows, unless, fleeing the startled post-coital couple when, after their gasps had quieted, you tried to sneak away but were heard as you began to pedal and the guy gave chase, you happened onto Centertown Road just as the Toms came careening along. The half-empty beer can just missed my head, skittered and foamed in the gutter before me, so that I swerved and almost crashed before the chase began, the chase over even as it started, no turn I made sharp enough to lose the flashing high-beams, heavy metal, rebel yells, the Duster gunning its engine and squealing its tires behind me. All roads led to some arena where I could be run down or run off the road. I shot, in desperation, for the hairpin of the drive-through lane behind the bank, riding all out and at the last second zipping across, right in front of the Duster, and into the alley, the tires screeching to me that my father was onto something about linemen after all as the car did not follow but, instead, made a rubber-burning, banana-shaped turn into the other end of the drive-through lane so that all I could do was fly from the bike as it still rolled, duck through a gap in the fence and fade into the warren of back yards as the Toms took out their roid rage on my wheels.

Breathless, sweating, halfway home, unfamiliarly afoot, startled by the shutting door and mum beneath the mimosa, privy to the vision, Mary, Queen of Arkansas. It seemed not to be too early for dreaming.

# 3.

THE CROWD STARTED TO GATHER LATE SATURDAY AFTERNOON, in the lot by the athletic fields, the spot blackened by years of pep-rally bonfires. Some carried fuel for the fire while a small group of men in three-piece suits finished a teepee of wood. One squirted the pile with paraffin while others retucked their escaped tails, and arriving penitents laid their offerings on and around the pyre: black T-shirts with hellish insignia, record albums, paperbacks. Two bored firemen watched from where they leaned against their truck, parked beside the field house, sweating in their short-sleeved uniform shirts as the sun bleached the sky and heat shimmered over the pavement. My last jogged lap around the cinder track was dust and the shredded wheat smell of the toasted fields, but a change was coming. The breeze that had barely breathed through town as I retrieved my bike's wrecked carcass behind the bank that morning was coughing now, blowing itself into a real wind, and shadows were looming on the western horizon. The pennants strung over the Datsun dealership across the county road flapped, loud enough for me to hear them over my own pounding pulse.

Reverend Alan, First Baptist youth minister, comfortable in tan three-piece suit, the warm wind just another blow dry pass for his feathered hair, wagged a floppy Bible, index finger bookmarking a passage he would never need to look at, stepped before the pyre and spoke, saying, I knew without needing to hear, that while this bonfire of the vanities had been inspired not by him but by a congregant, a woman simply seeking the best for her family in a dangerous world, Mrs. Kramer come on up here, and there she was, too, the frosted-tipped, gray-teethed mother of a kid I vaguely knew, alarmed by the displays of devilry in the record store when she'd gone in to buy Kramer a record for his birthday, just a mother looking out for children, the community's as well as her own, who had seen the evil all around them and, unwilling to accept it, brought them all hither to this spot where they would, in the full view of the town and the Lord, fight it. There were cassette tapes, he pointed to a couple of teens in white, cross-bearing T-shirts, for those who wanted to buy a copy of his sermon on hidden Satanism in today's radio and TV, the proceeds going not to him, of course, but to the First Baptist Youth Crusade, and anyone needing a new T-shirt today after burning up a black one should know, too, that there were beautiful Crusader Tees on sale, $4.95 apiece or two for eight bucks.

She was standing on her own, far from the crowd around the woodpile, Mrs. Jansen, freshman English teacher at Payne High, shaking her head, having changed our week's reading to *Fahrenheit 451* because if people in Centertown were going to be burning books then we ought to know something about bookburning and, when reminded that it was really records that were to be burned, not books, she hoped the ministers and parents got up close and took a nice, deep toxic breath. Mrs. Jansen, from whose classroom walls a trench coated Camus glowered around a cigarette and a hatchet-faced Beckett threatened and a Baldwin shyly smiled at the fire next time, who beguiled in black from low neck to high heel, able to get away with anything by virtue of Bo Jansen, husband, fireman, first and foremost former

Pirates fullback, former second-string Longhorn, camp-cut Cowboys rookie who would, as anyone in town would tell you, have helped to beat the Steelers if the team had only kept him on. Bo was the taller fireman leaning against the flame-red truck, the one to whom Mrs. Jansen walked now, to whom she talked now, pointing at the parched brown grass and the popping pennants, the one who shook his head and shrugged, his eyes unwaveringly fixed on the fire-to-be until she stalked back to her place and, unnoticed by anyone else, took a cigarette from her purse and lit it, not smoking it for long, only a subtle puff or two, before she stepped onto the crisp, brown grass and dropped it.

Reverend Alan preached, saying: "And so, brothers and sisters, we are, as the people of the Lord always have been, beset by snares and dangers. The Enemy is watchful and inventive, and when we are not vigilant, we invite the darkness into our midst. We allow into our homes the insinuating voice that says first that we should relax, that tells us 'take it easy,' that allows us to 'do it' if it 'feels good.' And once we have softened our stance against the Evil One, once we have allowed the stern and truthful voice of our Lord and his Book to fade into the distance as we turn the volume up, then new voices make themselves heard, voices that say to us now not simply that we should relax, not simply that we should enjoy, not simply that we should enmire ourselves in the pleasures of the flesh, but, rather and worse, that we should bring our faith and allegiance over from the light to the darkness. And, just as in the Garden of Eden, when the serpent spoke with a forked and treacherous tongue, these voices sing to the innocent, they sing to the most vulnerable and gullible among us. Do they sing out loud and strong and true like the psalms of David or the prayers of Jesus, like the letters of Paul or the hymns of the church? Why no, brothers and sisters. The word of the worm is not a word that can withstand the open air and the light. He and his minions sing in code. They sing their songs backwards and lay the backwards song under an innocent one, just as witches of old did their evil by reversing the prayers of our Savior. They hide their malfeasance behind cartoons and comedy. They trick our youth, our future, into servitude and bestiality. And then, when the ground has been prepared, when the sneaking and crawling evil has rotted the defenses from the inside and peopled the citadel with insinuators and seducers, then, oh then, the Devil reveals something of his face and of his nature. Then the demons stand and shed their skins, they strip their glossy promises like pelts and show themselves naked and bloody, as they show themselves here on this pyre, in their true form of grinning and slobbering and raving ugliness."

The knot tightened around the minister, catching his words before the wind whipped them away and up into the gathering clouds, closer now as he stood in silence, head bowed and feathery hair blowing in his eyes, saying "When the people of Israel plighted their troth with their Lord, they made unto him, at times of celebration and at times of supplication, at times of penance and at times of cleansing, burnt offerings of the fruits of their fields and labors, of the beasts that were their wealth. And when the people chosen by the one true God came upon the idols and false gods of their promised lands, they did destroy those idols and consign them to the flames. And so it is that we today, brothers and sisters, have gathered before our Lord to cleanse and purify our homes by bringing out these tools of the

Enemy. And so it is that we here and now make an offering unto the Lord of the fruits and beasts and of the idols and the paraphernalia of wickedness in all its many forms. And as we light the match that will in turn light the fire that will consume these outward and visible forms of the evil that has sneaked into our homes, there to corrupt the innocent and to break down the defenses we have raised against the darkness, let us join together in prayer, speaking to our Lord as his Son, our Savior, taught us to pray, saying 'Our Father.'"

A born pedagogue, Mrs. Jansen let you run with something until it tripped you on its own. "There, their, they're," she would write in the margin, her corrections, in class as on paper, felt like flirting, her look as well as her looks tying adolescent tongues, and when their eloquence escaped them, her logic smoothly stung. And so it was only when Reverend Alan and Kramer's loving, distraught, determined mother lit the wicks of a couple of long wands used to reach the highest candles for Sunday services, he serious in vest and jacket as she revealed gray teeth in a grin and held up the flame for everyone to see, that Mrs. Jansen left her spot at the edge of the field and went to her husband and drew his attention to the little wisp of smoke that rose from where she had stood and gestured toward the paraffin-soaked pile of records and t-shirts atop the seasoned wood. The fireman rolled his shoulders back and shook his head, snapping something I could not quite hear, something that slapped Mrs. Jansen like a palm against the cheek, and strode over to stop the lighting of the pyre. Eye-beams shot like lasers back and forth across the parking lot, Kramer's mother staring at Mrs. Jansen who stared at her husband as the reverend raised his voice again to say the fire department's diligent concern for all their safety and the safety of the town had determined that conditions were unsuitable for the bonfire, saying, "The people of the Lord have done well to bring these materials for destruction and they will be destroyed indeed, though stuffed in garbage bags and dragged to the dump. This, though, is often the way of faith, and in our unspectacular attendance to our duties and obligations we live our life in the Lord, and so I'll see y'all tomorrow in the pews. God bless."

A few kids tried to take their things back from the pile but parents yanked them away as the wind kicked up and kept the Crusaders from getting their hymn going. The pennants flapped and soon there were only a couple of janitors shoving records and T-shirts into bags and Kramer's mother standing by the shrunken pile of devilry, her hair in frosty points. Mrs. Jansen glanced at the top of the bleachers and seeing me there seemed to wink.

With eyes in Centertown being, like the hailstones that were starting to pelt down, generally icy, hard, and likely to damage, you had to have havens, hideouts, and by day there were few to be found. Only the undeveloped patches, scrubby strips too negligible, narrow, or unprofitable to bother paving, fuzzed the landscape, odd interstices out of the way, spaces out of sight and out of time, the stretch of woods along each side of the ravine between the stadium and the back of a block of doctors' offices across the creek looking, as I ducked in, like the same ragged and brambly waste it had when Fats Crandall and I had first explored it sometime in second grade. A twig from our branch of the Trinity trickled through the ravine, whose depth showed that it must have run like a real river once, though now, with all the culverting and paving, it only rose above your ankles after a big storm. Generations of high schoolers had smoothed the rough edge of the woods that bordered Payne, gathering around one big sycamore to smoke safely off school property, tossing their butts six feet back onto sacred ground. One well-worn path led to the edge of the ravine, over which the same generations had tossed beer cans, burger wrappers, and each other; a side spur took the knowing down a shallower slope to the creek bed into which someone had pushed a Kroger cart, which lay there rusting in inches of muck. The rest remained a tangle of twisted live oak trees and grapevine, in the heart of which, where brush whorled in the apparent impenetrability of a cursed castle, lay the secret chamber, accessible only through a curtained opening Fats and I had missed the first dozen times we had walked by, furnished, after our labors, with a fallen-tree seat and an old foot locker.

 I hadn't been to the hideout since the last spring, hadn't spoken to Fats since we started at Payne either, and it was clear he hadn't hung out there for some time, no snack wrappers littering the leaf-swept floor and nothing in the foot locker but the tattered *Playboy* we had shared since finding it along the path, and a copy of *The Fellowship of the Ring*. Still, it was a place picked out by chance, the best available, nature imitating art, enclosed to keep unruly beasts out, though we knew we never had it fully for our own, finding, as we sometimes did, as I did now, the odd shed snakeskin. In its cheerful shade we could hear, from the scorched field they practiced on, the brazen band dinning the Payne fight song, and if it hadn't been raining I might have stayed. It was good to be reminded, after the adventures of last night, of retreats, redoubts, bowers and grots, of somewhere, anywhere, to hide.

Across the creek, emerging into the parking lot of Pleasant View Group Practice, where once in a while I went with a bout of strep throat and where once a year Dr. Kaplan probed my groin and made me cough, I saw the car. You didn't have to be a gearhead to know this car, even I could recognize a red Ferrari Testarossa though, with the rest of Centertown, I'd never seen one in real life: a sculpture, sleek and low-slung, lethal speed suspended, you could tell, until a spark brought it back to life. A doctor I hadn't seen before, sport coat over a shoulder, white lab coat casually carried in the other hand, sauntered across the parking lot, opened the car door, tossed the lab coat in and carefully hung the jacket over the back of the driver's seat, aware of my watching, every gesture a territorial spurt of spoor, a definition, demonstration, and indelible evocation of the phrase, one I had never understood before, "cock of the walk." The engine purred, smooth and feral, and when the car crawled across the lot and leapt out onto Pleasant View with a satisfied rubber screech, it was the cheetah taking down the impala on *Wild Kingdom* and the rest of my walk home felt like a forty-five on thirty-three.

4.

GABRIEL NIBBLES, RETREATS, ADVANCES *on a larger bit of cookie, scarfs and runs away, maybe to store it somewhere, comes back a little later but not too close. The king of the squirrels is cautious, still, though closer to the open window every night. Homework beckons. Doctor Seymour, during today's tutorial, pushed him to keep talking about the image in his essay. Say more about the snow, she said. Say more about the roses. Put together, polished, professional more than professorial. She is where you get your money's worth, though the intellectual sparring leaves him exhausted.* Why snow? Why roses? Do roses even bloom when there is snow? *(Had she not read the Louis MacNeice poem he referred to?)* And if so, must they be hothouse roses? *And if so, then they are artificial, and so what is behind this artifice?* That is the essence of the work, she liked to say: to get behind the artifice.

The squirrels are inactive after dark, though he hears, as he half wakes, turning and plumping the inadequate pillow, scritching and scratching near the window, closed to a crack now against the chilly night.

He is not sure whether his regular chess game with Willoughby, a saturnine argument against graduate school, scruffy, shuffling, and unkempt, counts as ritual or work. It feels a bit like both, work as he tries out the Emerson opening or the Bert Williams castle strategy, ritual as they silently set up the board. Even the dynamics of their game-time conversation smack of visits to an oracle. He poses the odd question— Are squirrels nocturnally active? Are there varieties of rose that bloom in winter?— *only to be met by Willoughby's insistent silence, the supercilious glance reminding him that this is a game of total concentra-*

tion before a knight is moved, fingers held atop the wooden whorls of mane, moved back, and, finally, a pawn across the board advances one square.

"Can roses grow during the winter?"

The dorm lounge where they play buzzes, always, with other conversations. They play in the quietest corner, more library than lobby, some long-dead alum's books shelved and available for perusal. He has taken a volume down from time to time, traced the title tooled on its leather spine, the indited lines, type bitten deep into toothed paper, preferring their heft and solid seriousness to the paperback class texts that fill the cases in his own room. During his first freshman months, he had tried, one book at a time, to shift some of this library from the lounge, where the books slowly moldered in disuse, to his room, not realizing that the prefects staged occasional inspections, embarrassed when he was asked, politely, to return the books so they would be available for others. An argument is rising at a table near the window, arcane, incomprehensible. He can hear all the words but cannot make sense of how the combatants are putting them together. This is a place of recondite vocabularies. He finds these to be among its charms.

"So what's the deal with family weekend? Seymour mentioned meeting my parents. Is that how this works? I thought they'd probably just take me out for lunch."

Willoughby glares as his rook falls, the broken wall, the burning roof and tower forcing an alteration in his strategy. He should have seen, though, that he was vulnerable. How can a pawn take you by surprise?

Prefects are finally called upon to calm the argument. The problem with arcana is that no one is sufficiently expert to referee, no one content to end in stalemate. Their game seems destined for stalemate. He cuts it short to make it to tutorial on time.

5.

"I HAVE BEEN INFORMED," Mrs. Jansen said, slight shadows lingering beneath lightly shaded eyes, handing out stapled mimeographed stacks, flick of tongue on thumb before each pinch of paper, "that we have deviated from the true course of rectitude as construed by the curriculum established for freshman English, and so," a definite wink at me now as she set the pile of poems on my desk, the scooped neckline of her blouse revealing a dusting as of powdered sugar at the top of her cleavage, "we will correct ourselves and turn our attention to what the state guidelines call the history of poetry in English from the Renaissance to the modern era, with attention to such elements of form as meter, rhyme, and figurative language." Against the chorus of groans, she descanted "Relax," her wicked grin a spark on my ever-ready tinder. "This is going to feel very familiar." The octave drop was a breath on the desire already, always, smoldering in my stomach. "The history of poetry is the history of guys trying to get laid." They tried for an hour, we watched them, cautioning coy mistresses about how worms would worry them when the winged chariot had run them down, dying if not living by love in a puddle of melted candle wax and the blood sipped by a lucky flea. We followed on our copied pages as she read from a fat anthology, the dull lines living in her voice, its hinting inflections, pauses, curl-lipped growls, and you didn't have to know what liquefaction was exactly to know that it was a great thing when it happened to Julia's clothes. She dismissed us with an order for a love poem of our own, and yes, of course, I could by all means borrow a copy of the book, she knew I'd like this stuff and if I only read one before tomorrow it should be this one, she flipped pages until she found the page and slipped in a scrap of last week's vocabulary quiz to mark it.

In the waiting room at Pleasant View Group Practice, I could make no sense of it. The note told me what "eremitic" meant and maybe that was me, wandering around town at night, planning improvements for the hideout in the woods, but the rest got lost in the grunts and curses I could hear through the podiatrist's door as the doctor earned his salary and more with tender mercies on my father's tragic toenails. These were awful to see when Dad peeled off his socks, twisted and yellow and viciously curled, their edges biting into angry red flesh. Fashioned from a tough substance you didn't know the body could produce, some horny remnant of ancestral phyla, trimmed with wire cutters when nothing else could get through them, the nails bit and their beds swelled with infection, pus caking and skin flaking away, screaming at the pressure of shoe leather and siren-singing for any nearby foot or obstacle to go ahead and have a stomp, to drive the hooked horns ever deeper into the underworld of inflammation.

On a page of my notebook I wrote the first line of my love poem. There were obvious things to write about a rose and I wrote them, the redness, the scent, petals patterned like a spiral leading from the outside to the depths you couldn't see unless you lay them back, gently, you had to lay them gently back, but all of these things were inert in my handwriting. I crossed them out and wrote that it was not too early for dreaming. The new doctor walked through, called, by the receptionist, as he walked by her window, Dr. Stark, listed, when I looked at the directory, as orthopedist, which, without a footnote, might as well have been "nature's patient eremite," but which must have been a way to earn enough for the Ferrari. The poem was for Mrs. Jansen, but it was about Nicole. What, though, did I know about Nicole? She had grown up half a mile away, had been two years ahead of me since I started school, had blossomed that summer into almost more than her bikini could bear, sunning by the Centertown pool, smoking in the shade outside the fence, had grown up half a mile away and walked through the same hallways as I did, but might as well have been a world away, me a moon watching as the chlorinated waves washed over her. I'd hardly ever heard her voice, had only ever seen her speak to Heidi D'Amico, though Heidi's voice I *had* heard, who hadn't, loudly laughing, complaining as she fiddled with a Bunsen burner, retaking freshman Physical Science, about boyfriends, teachers, detention for smoking in the bathroom, and asking, as I followed the experiment, how big this hickey was, holding her peroxide hair aside, asking, at the end of class, to borrow my notes. Inflamed, the podiatrist said, every time he took a look at my poor father's tortured toes. In flames. I closed my eyes and Mrs. Jansen leaned over my desk, black fabric gapping for a gape, the dusting of powder on the page of my notebook a fall of white snow on the pale stone of no hillside I had seen in this life, something like the cover of the book I'd borrowed.

"Fats Crandall got his books knocked out of his arm," I said, my father's wince not for Fats, Warren to parents, but for his right big toe as he pressed for a light in late-afternoon traffic, braking as the car ahead summed up the better part of valor as light went from newly red to red-too-long-to-run. "Football player named Scruggs came up behind him and just knocked his stuff out of his hand, knocked it all over the hallway."

"Jimmy Scruggs?" punching the accelerator and "Fuck" remembering too late the toe, and when I nodded he smiled and said that was one hell of a linebacker, Jimmy Scruggs. Crandall, coming from his locker after lunch, heading for three afternoon classes, loaded with a pyramid, the keystone *Warriner's English Grammar* slipping so he had to stop and fix it every few steps, the whole corridor catching on when Scruggs signaled with a smile to his buddies, some moving to one side and everybody watching from one corner of an eye the running start. Crandall sensed at the last second trouble coming up behind but before he could react Scruggs punched a big right fist into the stack jammed between belly fat and acned elbow. Grammar skidded to the end of the hallway, the place echoing with laughter as Crandall bent to gather up his scattered afternoon.

Hell of a linebacker, beefy and bearded Jimmy Scruggs, unmet by my old man, who, on the other hand, had hosted Warren Crandall at our house, had fed him burgers overcooked on the gas grill, bread and beef being two-thirds of Crandall's diet. Warren small-talked parents better than I did, even while beating me at chess, impressed them with his grades, so much that when I hit a skid in algebra they snapped that I should be more like that kid, he seemed to get things, could reel off the kings of England, presidents of the United States, countries and capitals and flags, while I ran around in circles, ovals, fine, ran around anyway. Up ahead, Heidi D'Amico's yellow Sunbird narrowly missed a darting squirrel and turned in at the 7-Eleven, Nicole Rose in the passenger seat, cigarette hand perched on the side mirror, the first I had seen her since the night I had seen her. "Hell of a linebacker," turning fast into our street. Under his breath, he wondered what the hell kind of name Fats was anyway?

Home-game Fridays, Centertown shut down. A pep rally pre-empted our last class and even football skeptics filled with spirit as the fight song roiled and rammed against the gym walls, was thrown back on itself to double and double again, the noise a living thing, trumpets and snares in a demonic hormonal roar exploring the twin logics of love and annihilation. Sore-throated and spent, students retreated to their rooms to recover and prepare. Cheerleaders primped and vomited, while the team warmed up with desultory cruelty. Everyone took off early to gird or grill their loins. I dawdled in the woods, October having finally broken the heat, a breeze knocking and scraping through the trees, rattling the browning leaves. In the hideout, I read Mrs. Jansen's notes on my homework. I should come up with more lines of my own and turn the record player off. I should write less about snow on mountains, there being neither here for observation, and should try a stanza about what I could see right here in Centertown. A dead tree hidden by grapevine in the ragged patch of woods between the football field and the doctors' office, a ragged scrap of fading pink panties stuck in the muddy creek.

A factual report on what I observed in Centertown. Noumena, pneuma. The swell of skin beneath cotton, linen, lace, silk, satin, polyester, rayon, blends of every kind and color, swell of breast against bra, against bathing suit, sudden and ubiquitous, smoke rising in tendrils, leaked from glossed lips to wreathe, entangle, rise into the nimbus puffing, building always in the wide suburban sky, spirit spilled, visible breath into breeze, blown away to fade, lingering still in the strand of dark hair pulled behind an ear, in the faint moan as hands hefted, held, palms pressed and subtle thumbs stroked, in the whisper of a page. Sex in shed skins, darknesses moving in darkness, friction sparks and slick salts, everywhere, everyone, moans pressed and drawn, twisting and rising like smoke, cresting, breaking, emanating from some place beyond control, beyond awareness, everyone, everywhere it seemed, but me, my skin burning for the touch of fingers not my own, inflamed, desire a fire consumed with what it fed on, fourteen a freakish creature from some ancient bestiary, three-legged, flame-skinned, breathless in the swirl of breath and breasts, a mobile nerve, exposed.

    I wrote six lines about the leaves as they browned and floated, then dawdled in the woods until it seemed safe to emerge, the rallied troops resting or rendezvousing in their halls or armories, until I might be late to my own house, to the cookout my father was throwing for his coworkers at P&C Office Supply, Pasco and Clifford and the other salesmen, then climbed up from the ravine to find the red Ferrari parked in its spot, far from the office door, athwart the lines, taking two places, space all around it, a sculpture, gleaming, and beside it the new doctor, lab coat nowhere to be seen, in khakis and pale purple shirt and darker purple knit tie and on one arm Mrs. Jansen, toward whose ear, as I emerged, he leaned as if to whisper.

    "Well, hello William," Mrs. Jansen said, a pillar of light and air appearing suddenly between them and the doctor's hands casually in the pockets of his khaki pants. "Let me introduce you to an old friend who's just moved to town. William, Paul. Paul, William."

The doctor's grip was strong and longer by a beat than mine so that he held me, trapped and limp, and when Mrs. Jansen said again they were old friends we all three heard the repetition in it, the words fainter the second time around, as if they had been washed. An orthopedist and did I know what an orthopedist was, well, if I studied Greek roots I would be a step ahead for senior year, but what it meant was one who made the children—*pedes*—right—*ortho*.

"Sports medicine," Stark said, but he didn't mean like the high school's training staff, butchers with Band-Aids. "Karen what's the Greek for that?" Mrs. Jansen smiled a hmm and leaned against the car. The doctor took her hand and pulled her from it, glanced to make sure nothing had been dented, scratched, marred, his lips pressed tight to say this was not the first time, they had talked about this. The roots, she explained, pulling her hand away and crossing her arms over her chest, would be "physic" or "medic," probably. He worked with knees, Stark told me, strong but structurally delicate. How were my own, now, after climbing up from the creek, after sneaking up on them? "Not sneaking," Mrs. Jansen said. "Short-cutting from the track that's just," chin jutting, "across there, through the trees." She turned to ask me whether I had been running.

"Runner?" Stark said. "Which event?"

"Four hundred," I said. He whistled.

"Brutal," he said. Mrs. Jansen asked how it was brutal.

Sprints, the doctor told her, were all mechanics, and distance runs were strategy. But the four-hundred meters was nothing but guts, an all-out once around the track that, if you did it right, if you did it the way you had to, left you with nothing at the finish line. "Brutal." Mrs. Jansen didn't figure me for brutal, sensitive as I seemed. Looks could be deceiving, Stark replied, and he asked about my stride. I should pay attention to my stride. You wanted everything to work together, everything to go the same direction, no torsion in the fine structures, no stresses on the tendons and ligaments. If I had a minute, he could show me, but I had to go, Pasco and Clifford would be getting to the house, and Mrs. Jansen looked at her watch, saying she needed to get moving too, her husband had the night off for the game, his last night of freedom for a while because he was rotating onto nights. "He ought to get hardship pay," Stark said, and I agreed that a fireman should, they were heroes, sort of, and the smile Stark flashed at me then was lightning splitting a fine old tree, one of the century-old cottonwoods by the disused Centertown cemetery.

"Oh, Bo's a hero, all right," Stark said, and Mrs. Jansen said that what he *was* was a city employee with a demanding schedule, and she'd better get home Did I want a ride? I did. In the Silver Supra, a muted trumpet poured ice in smooth sheets over a warm, syncopated pulse, a sound like none I had ever heard. "Miles," she said, and I said that it wasn't that far, and she went on that she loved Miles, that was one thing about college, you discovered loves you couldn't have imagined in your life before, loves that went with you forever afterwards, bliss was it in that dawn to be alive and to be young was a lonely impulse of delight driving toward tumultuous wild nights, wild nights, and I should promise her that I would go away to college, somewhere covered with ivy and full of European profs and not come back to Centertown. College was where she had met the corrector of children? Oh yes, and he had been so driven. That car. He had set his sights on that car from before she knew him and when she first went to his room in that Austin dorm there had been a magazine photograph of the Ferrari tacked up over his desk, he would look up from memorizing bones and know that the work was work toward that object of desire.

"You wouldn't believe how I had to compete with the image of that car for his attention." But, she went on, the trumpet breaking now into icicles and shards, junipers shagged and roughly glittering spruces, that had been before she had met Bo. The important thing was that I should know there was a world beyond what Centertown suggested. I was sensitive and smart and this town could be hard on sensitivity and smarts. We worshipped the wrong things around here, had the wrong heroes. There was in her perfume something of wintry evergreen, in her eyes the green of pines hurled up in waves and washed out in the sea, and the slight salt of seawater I had never yet seen or tasted in her voice, salt drops gathering for some reason in the corners of her eyes as she turned where I said we had to and steered us to my street, drops that she blinked away, smiling and waving at my father and his friends where they stood smoking out front of the garage, staring at the Supra as it dropped me for the pregame barbecue and departed for her house in Arden Court.

"They got this boy," Pasco was saying, "got to watch out for him, now."

"Greased pig in the backfield," Clifford said. "Greased lightning in the open field."

A chorus continued as I moved across the yard: *That kid could put up twenty on his own if we don't shut it down. You got to blitz early, get in there and rattle things around, rattle that boy's teeth in his helmet so he don't know where the holes are. Don't talk to me about some I tol' ya towel heads. I ran all the way to the store and back. I ran so fast my mama couldn't catch me. I ran this and that. Only bearded sumbitch I care about is Santa Claus. This ain't the six 'clock news, it's Friday night football. Can't let them get a rhythm, they get a rhythm you're in for a long night, but you hit that boy early enough, you hit him hard enough, he's gonna hear bells when he gets the ball. Now we got offense, don't get me wrong, but it's a ball-control offense, a possession offense, a ten-minute touchdown drive offense. It'll eat up the field like a half-starved goat, but it'll eat it slow. Carter, don't talk to me about that sumbitch Carter. You know who ought to run for president? Tom By-God Landry, that's who. You get behind early cuz you let that boy of theirs run loose, you got a lot of grass to eat up fast. You got to shut that thing down, get in there and rattle the rhythm, then you can saddle up behind those Toms and chew up turf.*

Barbecue fingers sucked and wiped, beer cans drained and crushed, the caravan wound to the stadium, October evening dry and cool, smoke rising from the stands, hot grease in the snack bar, hot grass on the field. Mrs. Jansen high up, one hand in the hand of Bo the hero while the other waved at me, impossible to imagine, now, Karen Phipps, as she would have been then, Longhorn coed, lit tutor taming the Centertown savage, a sophomore backup running back, tutor buttoned up in a button-down, stern behind the glasses she slipped on to read from the big book, closeted in a carrel, surprised by joy, seduced by, there the vision failed, something they read together, something she read to him, seduced by, there it was, something on the page that rose into the air between them and transformed bestial Bo, whirled them around the stacks and into each other's arms, a better story than the likelier one, in which young Mrs. Jansen, Karen Phipps as was, falls for the hot jock just like all the girls do. From the top of the bleachers, I could look down on the parking lot and see, leaning against Heidi D'Amico's yellow Sunbird, Nicole Rose courted by rope-muscled dropouts, coolly half-smiling as she ashed her cigarette, another reality impossible to reconcile with what I almost thought now that I had not seen. Friday nights in the fall brought to its keenest edge the need to be touched, the need, unmet, I could escape only by exhaustive acquaintance with the night. And sure enough Payne over South Arlington by three with just two unnecessary roughness flags, my father saying, on the way home, that *that* was the way to do it, that was some real football, and my mother wondering why those kids didn't take their hats off for the national anthem, didn't anybody love their country anymore? And when they were in bed, their muttered repetitions repeated into muttered snoring counterpoint, after half an hour watching the old movie show on Channel Eleven, Cary Grant and Deborah Kerr parted by circumstance and kept from the top of the Empire State, half an hour envisioning Mrs. Jansen suffering the predations of her Bo, recalling Nicole Rose's tender touch, her soft sigh under the orange glow, I wandered.

Arden was far from my neighborhood, a cul-de-sac in the pretty tangle around the library: Stratford, Elsinore, Avon. Ours was an older neighborhood, second-generation, brick ranches rather than the steel-sided bungalows built for the plant's first workers, smaller than the homes that had grown up for managers and commuters. A history of Centertown by street names started with the trees—Oak, Maple, Cypress, Chestnut—that branched northward from the old highway. After the forest, the institutions, the clotted intersection of Church and State, the byways of Chapel and School. Our neighborhood dated from the aspirational age, from my house on Harvard Street I could turn right and pass the neglected yards and the chain-linked precincts of Columbia to get to Dartmouth, where Nicole Rose lived. I went left, instead, and cut through the park at the dead end, shuffling through the brown leaves recently fallen from the biggest trees, their dusty dead smell wafting through the cool, went right up Nicole's street, right along the curb before her house, not even bothering to stay out of the streetlights' semicircles, seeing nothing that was not there to see and the nothing that was, the no sign at all of Nicole in the porch shadows or under the mimosa, walked to the corner and turned around, a Peeping Tom for anyone to see, a stalker in the night noticeable to any open eye, and saw, on passing by again, the one illuminated window, pale light falling in a rhombus on the narrow side yard, and here, if I had been a Peeping Tom, I would have sneaked right up and peered in at this bathroom, bedroom, broom closet, but, cowardly, I stood instead for a few seconds hoping to see a shadow pass before the light and, when nothing moved, even the breeze through the dry leaves, I retreated in the still silence, knowing that if I looked too hard at that light or at the darkness that comprehended it not, I would see nothing but myself staring back, eyes burning with frustration.

I rarely knew what the fight was about. It would, when I came home to it or awakened to it or startled from my homework to it, be already full-blown, a sudden summer thunderstorm like those that swept through, a breathless afternoon all at once dark, the sky gutted and pelting hail. The fight song was symphonic, dark and protracted, long phrases punctuated by a dish against the wall, a fist punched through the thin plaster skin in the hallway. Even when driven underground, it would buzz beneath the surface of a drive or dinner. That fall, the fight song was in heavy rotation, my father coming home each evening ready to explode, my mother moody, bristling as she stood at the sink and scrubbed a pan or started to cook, and why wasn't dinner already done, but why should it be when he was late the last three nights, and as the clouds gathered and the brasses warmed up I sought my room or the garage and my bike's unending repairs, before the thunder struck.

Parents fought. In our neighborhood, houses separated by tiny side yards and life lived by the grill out back or around the car as it lay disassembled in the driveway, we all heard plenty of parental argument, all learned to tune it out, to ignore the sudden silence after a smack. But when it was your own folks, when one or the other always wanted to use you as a weapon or excuse or casus belli— "He's not contributing, he ought to get a job, what will he ever amount to anyway, why does he run around in circles?"— you would just as soon skip it. Sometimes, I'd be stuck, pinned in place with a snarled "Where the hell are you going?" But whenever I could, I'd slip out while their attention was on each other and their anger. I did a lot of roadwork. Normally, I hated roadwork, every yard after the four-hundred-and-first a grim two steps that might have measured the distance to death. But when, one midweek mid-October dinner time, the faint strains of the fight song started, I laced up and hit the streets, leaving my neighborhood and heading southeast, away from town and toward the plant and the old county road. Beyond the factory parking lots, a couple of farms had hung on, but not much else was out there and it was the most convenient way between precisely no two places, only the rare car to force you back into the grit and broken glass on the shoulder and mostly just acres of fenced pasture. The old town cemetery, not the one you would get buried in now but the original, where the early settlers had buried their dead, crumbled into its weeds a couple of miles from my house, the overgrown patch of long dead Centertown, each of the hamlet's rude forefathers forever sleeping in his narrow cell, a useful landmark, time to turn around.

I rarely knew what the fight was about. It had been going on one way or another since before I was born, had started, maybe, in the prehistory of their marriage, back when the old man was young and taken with the lonely refugee from Nebraska, to which, he sometimes shouted now, he'd like to send her back and maybe she could look up her old stepdad if she didn't like things in this, his, house. With no reason to hurry home, they'd just about be hitting their stride now, I walked through the ever-open ornate gate of rusted wrought iron to linger with the dead. Most of the stones dated from the first half of the century, the eroded dates on a few, the oldest, from the 1880s. Beloved father mother sister wife daughter of ashes to dust returneth, some of the verses half hidden by leaves fallen and riding the rising tide of weed. In a shady quadrant far from the road, a patch of the cemetery so dark as the autumn sun was setting that you could read nothing on the smoothing faces, stood a bunch from 1919, when the flu tore through town and almost filled the fenced-in area. I shivered, the breeze cold through my sweaty shirt and jogged back to life, was halfway from the corner to my own driveway before I caught the oddity. My mother's car was gone. It was normally my father's pickup that tore from our driveway, to return only long after we'd gone to bed, grumbling for a second after the key had killed it, my father grumbling too as he scraped at the knob until a lucky strike landed in the lock, catching his stumble against the coat rack in the hall, just as it was normally the next day before my mother drove to Target and soothed herself with flipping through blouses on the racks, picking up a new set of glasses since a couple of the old ones had been shattered. Inside the house, nothing strange, the president maundering from the television, the poor Shah just needing a place to wash up and be sick, my father breathing from behind the *Star-Telegram*. I had almost made it to my room before he called me back to ask where I had been.

"Running," I said. "Coach has us putting in a bunch of miles on our own."

And where was I going now? To my room to prove a theorem, to find the causes of the Civil War, to finish reading Aristotle for English, but not, he said, wincing as he shifted, the trauma of his toes now redly, rawly calling to be recognized, until I had cleaned up the kitchen, and when I asked if I could change my sweaty shirt first the injunction not to sass sent me, chants from Tehran at my back, to the dinner dishes still on the table, pans still on the stove, grease and butter varicolored pastes and, on the wall opposite the sink, a bent nail sticking from the spot where, when I had left, a picture of the three of us had hung, an enlarged snapshot from the Rangers game we'd gone to for my tenth birthday. This, its plastic frame now bent and its glass cracked, lay on the floor, and under and around it rose a pile of jagged shards that had, that afternoon, been every drinking glass in the kitchen. Little divots pocked the wall, some with glass fragments still sticking in the paint and plaster. Shoveling the glass up in the dustpan, I could hear my father stand and, cursing, limp off to the bedroom, his stomped toes torturing each step, the closing of the door between us lost in the crystal river as I tipped the dustpan into the garbage. Pity and terror. There was the glass dust to sweep up, the table to clear, the dishes and pans to wash. *Hamartia, catharsis,* and conclude with the restoration of order after its interruption.

6.

A BASTARD'S LOVE MIGHT BE REDEEMING, though whose redemption was at stake I couldn't say, watching, again, light shining into the side yard, hesitating in my hiding place across the street, having, on past nights, finally headed home without approaching the rectangle of illumination. Tonight, I had decided when I left the house, the riots televised from Tehran for the quiet of our Ivy League streets, I would approach the shrine. There were, though, as I now discovered, obstacles, an ornamental shrub beside the window, its leaves concluding in sharp points. Standing beyond its scratchy grasp, all I could see at first was a room that might be anybody's room, lamplight casting on pale walls patterns of shadow. Closer, though it cost a little blood, and there was the skinny Springsteen on *Darkness at the Edge of Town*, blown up to poster size, positioned to stare across the room at, as I could see with a little more scratchy struggling, the bed whose head-end lay in the pool of light shed by the lamp and on which, sitting in profile, her back against the wall and a textbook on her knees, staring at the page and idly holding to her lips as though it were a cigarette a pen, Nicole Rose studied. I studied Nicole, icon and altar, outward and visible, sign and wonder, study in chiaroscuro, wondering whether it would be worse to be caught by some idle sideward glance she might cast or to be consigned to this eternal unknown watching, the real worst, however, coming in the form of Hector's Camaro, whose distinctive rumble I heard now and to whose bumper I now saw myself bound, dragged through Centertown, the hurdle that would carry me to the Bottoms to be drawn and quartered for peeping the man's sister.

A sprint, that second, might get me to the park before the Camaro turned the corner, but, hemmed in by the spiked shrub, I missed that chance. Quicker, Nicole, hearing the Camaro at the same time, shut her book and jumped to the bedroom door, turning the switch in the knob to lock it as she turned back to the bed, turned off the lamp, and disappeared into the sudden dark. As Hector's headlights swept the yard, all I could do was shrink against the house. The Toms were a threat you could imagine escaping, just a mass of muscle and meanness, but Hector was lethal, cut and quick, his butterfly knife's profile faded into the back pocket of his jeans, captain of the drop-out crowd that gathered at the Dairy Queen, gunning engines at stop lights and racing through the Bottoms, and now he was going to catch me lurking by his sister's window in the middle of the night and he was definitely going to kick my ass. The Camaro sped from the corner to the Roses' curb and parked facing the wrong way, lights dying with the engine's exhalations and Hector was out, with neither a glance nor a thought for the side yard where I squatted, and, with a slam of the car door and a few steps up the walk, inside the house. Reprieved, no curfew rung around my neck for now, I slunk through the hot metal haze of custom muffler, mocked by the click of the cooling engine, not knowing that it might have been a better thing to have been caught and stopped then, the having got away with the night's spying the first dose that hooks the unsuspecting and paves the pathway to addiction.

I would go back on other nights, but there were, before the nights, the days to be gotten through, so many yellow and orange flyers tacked to telephone poles all over town and stuck beneath the windshield wipers of cars in the Kroger parking lot, advertising Reverend Alan's upcoming series of sermons on satanic temptation, the threats to our youth, and how to combat the seductions of a permissive, profane culture, autumn leaves blown on the whirlwind, signs of the signs foretold, the end times now doubtless upon us and those who would save themselves from tribulation urged to get their houses in order. We were invited to hear the Word and join our voices in prayer, the months-long revival to culminate on the first Sunday of Advent in the completion of the postponed Bonfire of the Vanities, to be built and lit in safety, in a space set off from all inflammables, under the approval and supervision of the Centertown Fire Department, and fire, Mrs. Jansen said, was a metaphor we would often encounter, especially as a figure for desire, for fire was hot and weren't we all hot for something. Someone.

"Fire is pleasure," she said. We craved heat when we were cold and didn't it feel good when we got it, but too much heat, like the classroom on this Indian summer afternoon, the A/C off after the last week's cooler weather, Mrs. Jansen fanning herself with a manila folder, the heat seeming to come from inside her, a red glow rising from her chest to her cheeks, well fire could get too hot, and then desire destroyed, the warmth of pleasure rose to a burning. We got that, right, the want too much, a fire out of control, want becoming need as a tickle becomes an itch, desperate as an itch became a burn. Flames could get by, for a while, on a little fuel, a little air, but if you fed them, then they could flare up, spread out, take all that they could get, and if the fire finally got all that it wanted?

"Fire consumes its fuel," Mrs. Jansen said, powder pale on the blush of her breasts. "It burns up what it eats until there's nothing left to burn and when it's done it dies itself and when it's dead there's nothing left but ash." Powdery dust over the pale skin of her chest and in the cleft some tiny clumps where grains had gathered on a drop of sweat, what would it taste like on my tongue, how would it feel, a paste on the back of my teeth, the pages of my notebook, as class ended and we gathered up our books, scribbled over, around triangles and the Gadsden Purchase delicate dustings of snow I had rarely witnessed on the slopes of mountains I had never seen, and then Fats Crandall got himself scalped.

Scalping was one of the lesser sports the Pirates took up between Fridays, the Toms descending on their targets like a hand from the heavens. Exactly like a hand from the heavens, the act of scalping simply the rapid descent of a beefy, muscular hand onto the upper back side of the victim's head and, at contact, the closing of beefy, muscular fingers around a hank of hair and, finally, completing this quick and continuous movement, the follow-through (fingers still grasping hair) so that a fist full of yanked-out strands was held aloft as the victorious hero called out "Scalped that faggot!" and his cohorts in reply joyously echoing "Scalped that faggot good!" We simple villagers went about our business in the wake of these attacks, just glad the victim had been someone else. I had suffered a scalping of my own back at Centertown Junior High, some Pirate-in-training getting in a practice shot before rising to big leagues, and had discovered that the cruelty of this game lay not in its pain (though it hurt like hell) nor in the humiliation of being brought to tears (though it was humiliating, impossible to stop the tear leaking from your eye as you stumbled under the blow), but in the act's premeditated preface, the scalper walking halfway down the hall with his hand hovering over the victim's head, alerting the assembled and creating in the victim, through some subtle change in gravity, some occult power in the scalp nerves to detect a threat, the presence of a hanging hand, inchoate dread before the execution. I had felt that atmospheric shift, suspected, flung my eyes around for an escape, and started, involuntarily, to turn and confirm, when the smack, the yank, and thunderous cry pitched me into a tear-blurred trip on the tile. "Scalped that faggot!" "*Scalped* that faggot *good*!"

Crandall's was textbook, the Tom following him down the hall, big right hand above the oblivious head, class ring turned stone down for an extra skull shock, bystanders making way. There was in the smirk on the Tom's face as he nodded to unseen confederates, nodded as if to an internal melody, neither malevolence nor apprehension but, instead, the serenity of an ancient Buddha, at one with the universe, borne on its vectors, powerfully unresisting, just a conduit for forces larger than himself, some universal justice beyond comprehension or resistance. In our deviations, steps angled from intended paths, we tacitly accepted the smirk's sermon, the Toms' cosmology, and on Crandall's face at the last second dawned awareness of the hand over his head, the hand swiftly swinging back and then, hard, forward, the ring's stone knocking on Crandall's skull so loudly it echoed on the pitiless white tiles. Crandall's face shattered, recomposed, a rictus of shocked agony, his books dropped and scattered at his stumbling feet, the Tom's fist rising, trailing strands of sandy hair, and to his giddily half-laughed "Scalped that faggot!" someone somewhere down the hall roared in reply, "Scalped that faggot good!"

Into the stunned silence, the crowd acknowledging the universe's hierarchy, each constituent grateful not to have been the head this time beneath the hand, Crandall, on his knees, whether fallen or in genuflection to justice beyond question, questioned, wailing "Why?" and thickening with shock the speechless corridor.

"Why?" The victim was supposed to suffer silently, to blink back tears and stifle the sob that rose in the throat. Every so often, one even achieved a kind of honor by shaking his head and forcing his lips to curl, ruefully accepting fate and allowing the assembled a relieved laugh.

"Why?" And at this third cry the crowd began to feel itself accused, the Tom himself not even having heard, already at the end of the hall, high-fiving teammates and on his way to after-school practice, though Crandall wasn't asking the Tom anyway, as everybody knew, to ask a Tom was like asking the August afternoon why it kept holding you beneath its hot thumb, blazing so you couldn't breathe. Tears wet Crandall's scandalous cheeks, his cry breaking at its highest point, falling away to husky sobs. Who did he think he was, letting that long and wordless wail echo up and down the corridor? And there, for the first time in ages, was Nicole Rose, masked and placid, impassively looking on, not seeing me seeing her, why would she with no idea who I was, until, her expression unchanged, she turned and walked away just as two teachers emerged from their rooms to see what all the fuss was, students walking to their lockers as if they had never noticed anything amiss, ignoring Crandall as he sat amid fallen knowledge and wept.

I picked up his grammar and handed it to him, Crandall looking up, no recognition in the red-rimmed eyes squeezed almost shut in his snot-smeared fat cheeks, held out to him the brick of declensions, asking if he was okay. He sat and raked some papers up, his shirt untucked and, when he leaned, riding up to reveal a roll of pale fat, my standing here revealing our relationship, tainting me with association. Still, he seemed so needful of a hand that I said again, setting the book down within his reach, "Are you okay?"

"I'm not," pressing his hand to the back of his head, and "I'm not," staring at the blood spots on his palm, and, when I asked if he wanted a paper towel, maybe, or maybe some ice, "I'm not," stuffing loose papers into a folder. "I'm not a faggot."

"I know," I said. "I know that, Warren."

He stopped, then, stopped picking up papers, stopped stacking folders and notebooks, stopped leaning so the fat pressed out between his shirt and the tight waistband of his pants, and looked at me for the first time, his face reddening, seeming to swell with something hot and nasty, to swell as if it would burst and flood the hallway with a poisonous tide. The scream he screamed then was the loudest, longest, strangest I had ever heard, a gale of anguish that you might have heard on some medieval battlefield as a sword plunged into someone's guts. The teachers hurried over, asking what was going on, asking me what I had done as I stumbled past, clustering around

Crandall as if he had hurt himself. My face felt like it had been slapped.

    Outside, the marching band was practicing, grinding into the grass the fallen yellow and orange revival flyers that had blown onto their field, pacing and pivoting and countermarching the paper back to pulp, the sun glinting on the bells of horns, mean little flashes here and there as the marchers sharply turned into crisp rim-shots, a few flyers floating up from their feet, rising to fall again at the edge of the woods, where, glancing now, I saw no Nicole among the smokers. There was, though, the low-slung savage grace of the red Ferrari slowly stalking the faculty parking lot, and there was, stepping from between two paler, tamer cars, Mrs. Jansen, both hands holding her purse's strap, glancing quickly toward the street and over her shoulder toward the school, prey for the predator, and then the Ferrari was upon her, the mouth of its passenger-side door soundlessly opening and, without ever having seen it coming, Mrs. Jansen was swallowed up by it, the car slowly U-turning and heading for the exit, no sign of my teacher there now so completely had the beast devoured her, only the doctor visible as he guided the creature to the street and turned it from the center of town and toward the highway access road, pursued, for a moment, by my gaze and the strains of the Payne High fight song.

7.

IT WAS LIKE A BUNCH OF THEM HAD DIED, students pallid and greenish, eyes sinking into dark pits, some with a dried froth of blood on their chins and in the corners of their mouths, died and been consigned to some circle of Hell that was the corridor of Payne, condemned to wander from bell to bell, clutching at theorems or the history of the United States. The Toms were frightening as Kiss, though no more frightening than when they stalked the hallway as themselves, sporting teased black wigs and trademark makeup, Knights in Satan's Service, as the Reverend Alan insisted, in his recorded sermons, certainly serving the Devil with the not-so-secret message of "Rock and Roll All Night."

Not everyone came to school in costume. A clutch of Alan's true believers wore buttons saying they were opting out of this pagan festival, and the reverend himself preached a sermon that morning on the athletic fields, assuring the faithful of the justice of their cause, the evil of their classmates, every red yarn wig or Nixon mask a tool of the Enemy. If you weren't among the popular elite or the self-exiling outcasts who came every year as the crew of the Starship Enterprise, you came in normal clothes to avoid attention. Tormented and helpless lonely children. Some of the teachers dressed as usual too, but others joined the fun. Mrs. Jansen was a witch. Under her spell, I loitered after school, pale and woebegone in the day's wake, awakened by whatever, in her enthusiasm, she talked about or lent or recommended, strange and wild and sweet stuff, unfamiliar and vast as the ocean after fourteen years of Centertown, and would have hung around her classroom that day, too, though, with the clocks now set back and darkness dropping at five o'clock, it would mean walking home with demons and haunts, but it was a Wednesday and Wednesdays, in the individual workout schedule Coach had handed out, were wind sprints and so, as the Hell mouth spewed its spawn into the cloudy afternoon, as Nicole Rose smoked with Heidi at the edge of the woods, I changed in the shabby locker room reserved for everyone but the football team and jogged around the track.

The first couple of sprints feel good. This is a little appreciated thing, your legs free as they aren't when you're putting in miles or working on drills, a reserve of wind behind you as you stretch out and drive over the forty yards so that your breath, as you pretend to break the tape, is not too hard to catch. You learn to enjoy the way the first sprints feel, as Sisyphus must smile as the stone rolls down the slope, because, after the first few, the sprints don't feel so great at all, and after a few more you end each gasping and wondering if you'll ever slow your heart back down, if the burning in your thighs will ever calm. You bend, hands on hips, on knees, and hope you don't puke, as I was bending, hoping, half a dozen sprints into the workout, when, glancing toward the woods at the oblivious Nicole, I saw the Ferrari slink into a parking spot by the end of the track. Doctor Stark got out, looking around the parking lot, looking like he was trying not to look like he was looking, then settled for standing in front of the car, his arms folded over his beige knit tie, and watching me. I pretended not to see him, took a couple of deep breaths, and sprinted down the lane in his direction, only obviously noticing him when, as I gasped and gagged back a hot bolus, he beckoned me over and asked what I was running from.

"Coach says," I panted, "work on my wind."

Well, if it was wind I was working on, then that was one thing, but if it was speed, he had noticed something, a little thing, but little things made big differences didn't they.

"Here," he cocked his arms like he was going to take off running. "When you pump your arms you do this," his fists slowly punching up and across his chest, his elbows pistoning out to the sides. "That's a cross-body motion when you want everything parallel, everything going the same way." He pointed at the Ferrari, saying, "Now that baby's engineered for speed and one thing those Italian engineers understood was the importance of everything moving along the same line of force." Did I know what a carburetor was? Did I ever, overhearing almost every weekend my father's cursing attempts to fix the sticking valve in his Chevy's. Okay, then, well carburetors were usually mounted vertically, perpendicular to the drive shaft. But when they designed this engine, those Italians mounted the carbs horizontally, so that all the energy produced worked along the same line and nothing would complicate the forward thrust.

"Here," he took my forearm and moved it back and forth so that my elbow brushed my ribcage and my fist pointed straight ahead. "Everything focused on forward momentum," he said, looking past me now. My eyes followed his and found Mrs. Jansen, black-coned witch hat in her hand, walking toward us and, beyond her, another set of eyes as Reverend Alan's anti-Halloweeners gathered by a white van that would take them to the alternative party at First Baptist. Kramer's mother stood by the van, too, ready to drive when the faithful were assembled. "It's like working for a goal," the doctor was saying. "You put everything toward that sucker and move in a straight line." He gestured at the Ferrari but his eyes were on my teacher, saying, "This car, for instance," saying how he had fallen for it the first time he saw one, had cut a picture of it from a magazine and tacked it over his dorm room desk, had looked up at it as he worked on every lab report, studied for every practical, to remind himself why he was working so hard. The youth group in their badges started singing, not a hymn I recognized, more like a bubble-gum love song to Jesus. That picture came along to med school, kept him up through residency and rotations. It had focused his momentum and conserved his energy, and everything in a straight line.

"Right," Mrs. Jansen said as she came up to us. "I think we've heard that story." What, was the doctor taking up coaching now?

"Some pointers," I said. "Keeping everything straight."

"Amen," the youth were singing now. "Amen, amen."

"Telling you how to cross the line?" Mrs. Jansen said.

"Oh yeah," Stark said. "And how to break the tape at full speed."

They didn't need for me to speak. The singers were louder and everyone from the track to the edge of the woods was watching them, singing now and loading into the white van, everyone but Kramer's mother, who was watching us instead and was not singing. My sweaty T-shirt clung to my skin. "You know," Mrs. Jansen said. "We've already got a track coach." But maybe, the doctor replied, there was an unsatisfied need still, and he would be happy to fill it. Too much running around in circles, he went on, not enough pushing to the finish. *Bold lover, never never canst thou kiss though winning near the goal.*

Mrs. Jansen reached into her purse and handed me a cassette tape, a homemade one, her writing on its label. "Autumn Leaves."

"Inspired by your writing," she said. "Let me know what you think." And, "We should let the runner run," she said to Stark. "Before he loses his momentum." The doctor was going to help her out, take her home after she left her car to get fixed, give her a ride. She needed a tune-up, Stark said, and she said again that he was just giving her a lift and she would see me in class tomorrow and enjoy the tape.

"Happy Halloween, kid," Stark said.

The gray Toyota slowly crossed the parking lot and turned out into traffic, the red Ferrari stalking after it, and after both went Mrs. Kramer's gaze. She turned and glanced at me then, crouching to start the next sprint, and started clapping and singing with the kids in the van, *amen, amen, amen.*

I wasn't a Peeping Tom. The first time I spied on Nicole Rose was an accident, right place, right time, and after that she was Mary, Queen of Arkansas. We can take this circus all the way to border. But if beauty is truth and truth is beauty, the symmetric property of equality being axiomatic, then what sense did it make to set up a pig's head on a stick and see it as a god while other kids were sharpening sticks into spears? I set the book down every time the doorbell rang and carried the big bowl of candy to placate evil spirits. There were contacts deep in Mexico, a consummation devoutly to be wished, and students were rioting against the great satan, my mother putting new glasses away in the kitchen and my father half watching the news. If, on the other hand, being was greater than seeming and being was equal to truth, which was equal to beauty, then, the transitive properties of equality and of inequality being axiomatic, being was equal to beauty and all was for the best in this the best of all possible worlds, Mars bars to skeletons in exchange for no egg smashed on the door, no toilet paper in the trees. She seemed a thing that could not feel, but I had seen her feel and which was real, being or seeming? Both were beautiful. And so, when the princesses and cowboys all deserted the streets and my parents made their sullen separate ways to bed and I realized halfway through the fourth song on the tape that the songs were all the same only this time it was in French, I had to walk out again and back again, autumn leaves blown around now with candy wrappers and rags of toilet paper fluttering over less fortunate front yards, drawn like a moth to the flameless light of Nicole Rose's bedroom lamp.

    She was lying on her bed wearing only a big T-shirt, her hair loosely pulled back, eyes closed, headphones pumping something from the turntable, her lips moving once in a while as she silently sang along to contacts deep in Mexico, to servants leaving or dreamers in the big top, waking, waiting, lying in bait, so that, her headphoned and me hypnotized by her lips as they subtly pressed and parted, the two of us sharing the sense of space out of sight, the privacy and protection not only of a room behind closed doors but, more than that, of insular experience, music in the specific solitude of nighttime, the fragility of safety, it was only as Hector's Camaro pulled up at the curb that I heard it, no tire squeal as he took the corner, no engine gunning as he parked, the car quiet as a big cat lazing after a gazelle dinner. Nicole never heard it at all. Suddenly and silently Hector was there, inside the bedroom, the door closed behind him, wearing a red foam clown nose, ha ha, Nicole hearing or feeling too late his presence, opening her eyes and yanking off the phones, crab-crawling into the corner of her bed and curling toward the wall. Hector was on her as quickly as he had come in, turning her easily onto her back, straddling her belly and pinning her arms to her sides with his knees, smiling when she shook her head, putting his index finger first against his own lips and then against hers, even as she struggled to pull her hands free, to buck him off with her hips and knees, a silent laugh when she got a hand free to slap at him, easily tucking it back between his knee and Nicole's hip. Her movements hardly distracted him as he pressed his palms to her breasts, kneading and squeezing through the thin cotton, smiling and closing his eyes, shifting his weight to free the T-shirt's hem and pulling the shirt up, revealing a quick and guilty glimpse of Nicole's nipple before he covered it, pinching and pressing at her with one hand while he shoved the other down the waistband of his jeans. It only took a minute and with a thrust and shudder he was done, wiping his hand on his thigh and standing as Nicole slapped and kicked at him. He put his finger to his lips again and waggled it at her. The red foam nose was still in place.

When he was gone, Nicole huddled in the corner of her bed and sobbed. Her back, fragile and bony, shook in spasms, stilled, and shook again. I watched until she lay quiet and seemed to sleep, a long time, and when I went to move away, my legs, stiff from standing motionless in the chill, tangled in the bush, my sweatshirt caught on a branch, and, startled, Nicole sat up, her wide eyes staring through the glass at me. I froze, waiting for the scream, but she just sat on her bed, knees drawn up in front of her chest, and looked at me looking at her. We stayed for a long time that way. She wiped her eyes and nose and looked and I looked back, our gazes meeting in a kind of touch, deep and intimate, saying something though I couldn't say what, recognition, understanding, tacit agreement, until, after a while, her eyes still on mine, she reached to her nightstand and switched off the lamp.

8.

DOCTOR SEYMOUR'S OFFICE IS LESS BOOKISH *than he would like. She lights the cigarette that always begins their meetings. A wall of books, she told him once, could be distracting. Their work together, she had said, might be understood as distraction from distraction by distraction. That's an allusion, but he has not yet figured out where it comes from. Where the allusion comes from, Doctor Seymour often says, is not important. The thinking that we do together in the space it opens up, that's the important thing.*

"You write that she brought roses once, roses blooming bright and red against the snow."

He doesn't want to talk about that image anymore. That's all right, they don't have to. What she is getting at is that she has, that very morning, struck upon something, a sticky image of her own that has helped to crystallize for her a way of talking about such things. Has he ever had a crumpet? Food, more even than the casual familiarity with books or films or music, slots him into his embarrassing provincial identity, but no, she says, few things are more provincial than crumpets, especially, as she had eaten this morning, crumpets smeared with something called Golden Syrup. Another substance with which he is unfamiliar. She herself has not found it in the supermarket here, brings a can – it comes in a green can, the kind with a lid you pry off with a knife blade or a spoon, which, after you've dipped some of the syrup out, gets gummed up and crusted – back with her when she goes to visit her widowed mother in Kilburn.

[59]

He had strawberry jam on toast this morning in the refectory, but it is unclear what all of this has to do with his essay, with roses on snow. There is, and if he has not yet come across it in his reading he will do soon, a famous bit of cookie crumbled in some tea that, when tasted, unlocks a powerful memory. It's how people talk about sensory memory, but madeleines weren't part of her upbringing. He hates to ask. He has to ask. Madeleines? They're biscuits, sort of, sort of cookies, buttery and cakey, quite delicious, not too sweet. But this morning, for her, the taste of Lyle's Golden Syrup on a crumpet warmed in the toaster oven catapulted her, with all the suddenness and violence that suggested, right back to the kitchen of a flat in Golders Green. The taste was sweet, yes, but such a peculiar sweetness, a caramelish burntness at the back of the throat, that it carried with it the occasion of its first appearance on her palate. Or not first, surely she had tasted the stuff before this, but the syrup's specific sweetness, the slow way it spread and grew and complicated across the surface of her tongue, the purity of it, delivered, that time, not on warm bread but, instead, directly from a spoon, spun somehow and in its spinning recreated the whole moment, the pale and peeling paint of that flat's small kitchen and the scrubbed deal table where she sat, the tremor across the cupboard when the Underground went through, her mother's tears and smile, just like those moments when the sun shines through falling rain, and the voice on the radio droning something she only understood when her mother translated, her voice shaking like the smile, like the teacups as the train passed far beneath them.

"*The war is over, pet. All over now.*"

There are, then, a couple of ways to think about a crucial image or impression. One, the way she had been suggesting in their last tutorial, would be to distil from the image its properties. To get at the question of why roses, why snow, why the two together, one might list those things peculiar to roses, to snow. Redness, fragrance, fragility, perhaps. Perhaps boldness. Whiteness, coldness, purity, sterility. And in the collision of the qualities, you might, with some interpretative pressure, reveal some broad— some universal, even— significance. On the other hand, though, and this was what had come to her when she'd tasted the syrup this morning, one could dwell instead on the unique associations the image might have for the one perceiving or recalling it.

"I have a friend who tastes Liverpool in Lyle's, the burning sugar flavor of the city's air when the sugar works are in full fire, but for me it is that morning, always, under whatever has accumulated since in all the mornings or teatimes when I've tasted Golden Syrup."

What, he wonders, does she know about squirrels? Is there any chance that they, like birds, are psychopomps of sorts? He has been watching them running around the courtyard and the highest, thinnest branches of the trees outside his dorm-room window, and they have, it seems to him, some spiritual sense. She glances at her watch and says she doesn't know much about squirrels, but what made him choose Gabriel as the name for the big one? Is that part of his suspicion that they might have something to reveal? To announce?

9.

THE END-OF-SEASON HOMECOMING GAME BONFIRE was a tradition as old as Payne itself, the very first graduating class having set a small blaze going to warm the team and supporters before they all set off to be humiliated by Trinity, the pyre now rising since midweek in its dark-burned patch of parking lot, site of every annual *auto-da-fe*, built between the end of school and the early sunset by cheerleaders and the booster club. Everyone came to the homecoming bonfire, I'd gone to my first as a baby. Everyone showed up early, crowded close to hear the coach's megaphoned speech. It was better a little way back, you couldn't see the cheerleaders dancing by the flames but you could see their shadows cast tall and threatening on the high gym wall, shamanic goddess figures for the savages to worship. My parents, truced and entreatied for the evening, worked their way through the crowd to get close to the fire while I wandered the edges where the fire truck was parked, Bo Jansen sternly watching from over the wire-brush mustache for any spark that might alight on an unwelcome spot, for any sign the flames were rising out of control, the Pirates' eternal enmity for this week's rival, the assembled having hated East Underarm or North Malebolge always, even if hearing of them for the first time now, tending to combust in unpredictable ways. Not a curlicue of smoke, not a glow of something smoldering on the tarpaper caught Bo Jansen's practiced eye, but he watched, and, following his gaze, I saw, too, the rough beast slouching toward the un-railed edge of the gym roof.

Shadows leapt against the wall, hung for the magic moments there, suspended on thermals of hate, the savages shouting, drum-driven and powerfully tromboned, dancing around the flames, chanting for blood, the Toms in their jerseys taking it all in, their due and duly delivered obeisance, nodding and grinning, preparing for the climactic moment when, before the flames could get beyond its toes, they'd tear down the hanging effigy and quarter it, tossing the paper-stuffed limbs onto the flames only after ripping them to fragments. The high priest had just ascended the altar, bullhorn in hand, to deliver his homily, when a high-pitched scream from above shut him up, shut up the band and the chants and cheerleaders too, and we all stared up then, even Nicole, whom I now saw in profile nearer the fire, being lined up for a shot by the yearbook photographer, to see Fats Crandall standing on the precipice, shouting for everybody to shut up. Only the fire ignored him, chewing and licking at its fuel, gulping, ravenous, as Crandall ranted his own sermon on our collective sins.

"Look," he shouted. Look at how we perned and rumbled, worshiping brute strength and nothing else, and look at him, fat and shitty at sports. Who cared that he could play the clarinet, that he knew the capitals of every country in Africa? Did we even know how many fucking countries there were in Africa? What kind of society was this that punished you for being smart? What kind of school, for Christ's sweet loving fucking sake? All of us looked down on him but we were looking up at him now, weren't we, and we should all take a look at what he thought of us, what he thought of our stupid fire and stupider athletes. Crandall fumbled at his crotch and then it was only when the people nearest the wall retreated that word spread: that fat sonofabitch was pissing on the pep rally.

I was alone at the margin of the crowd, remembering long summer days in the thicket with dwarves and elves and Playmate breasts and package after package of the Little Debbies Crandall stole from home, thinking not me, not me. I was alone in this crowd, Crandall's best friend since grade school, his wild eyes not recognizing me, or, worse, recognizing me too well, just before he loosed that scream in the hallway. I was alone now. Even the firemen were gone. The ignored fire ignored, the crowd rumbled. For all his life, we had made fun of Fats, shoved him to the side, stared and smiled and snickered, if we paid attention to him at all. Well, he was done with that. Attention must be paid. He was done with that, he was done with us, he was done with everything, his voice breaking, spitting sharp fragments of screech, a hard rain of broken glass on the crowd, and if we wanted a savage ritual, we could have a sacrifice too, a blood sacrifice, and if we liked watching him get scalped then see how we liked watching his skull smash on the concrete and he hoped to see us all in Hell.

"Scalp that faggot," Crandall screamed. "Scalp that faggot good!"

And then, from out of nowhere, two arms came around Crandall from behind and a body familiar with the physics of it tackled him to the flat roof. We couldn't see anything up there until Bo Jansen stood up and waved and shouted that it was okay, Coach should get back to his pep talk.

"Lotta folks," the coach fed back through his megaphone. "Lotta folks talk about football and call our young men heroes."

He wasn't going to argue with them, he'd seen what they did on the field, but "Y'all just saw a real hero in action, how 'bout that, how 'bout that." The firemen, once Coach was into his speech, led Crandall, sobbing and stumbling under a blanket, around the crowd and to their truck. Nicole was gone from where I had seen her before, her picture, a shadowy profile against the flames, captured for the yearbook. The cheerleaders cheered then and the crowd chanted along, the shadows heaving on the wall, the Toms tearing into the effigy, everyone happy to get back to thinking about nothing but beating the hell out of Colleyville.

Let it be postulated that the connection from any given point to any other given point is a straight line. My bike finally fixed, I rode to school that Friday morning, no need for creek-bed shortcuts and I could leave the fat English book in the hideout for another time. For the first time in weeks, the world moved past my shoulders at the right pace. All right angles are equal to one another, and non-parallel straight lines, if extended far enough, converge. The unrest in Iran was growing and American diplomatic personnel would be withdrawn if the situation began to threaten their safety, and, as Chapter Six showed we read it silently throughout the period, answering the review questions in writing if we finished, sectional tensions rose in spite of efforts at compromise and the relief produced by territorial expansion. Around any point, a circle may be described, with any length of radius. By the time I got to English, the boys were set on killing Ralph and Piggy and Mrs. Jansen looked like the day had beaten her up. All that anyone talked about was her husband's heroism. After everyone had left, I walked up to her desk to thank her for the tape. She had hoped I would like it, she said, and hoped I didn't mind the joke, it was just that I seemed, in all the practice paragraphs and sonnets we were writing, to have a special fondness for autumn leaves. We didn't really get the kind of leaves people thought of, did we, the summer's end, when it finally came, simply turning them all brown and the trees, relieved, dropping them overnight. The white powder paled the skin of her chest, the tops of her breasts, a fall of snow on mountains I had never visited. It was clear that I should go somewhere with a real fall. I would love to, somewhere, I told her, with mountains, too, dusted with snow, but where would that be. She said maybe New England, or New York, not the city but upstate somewhere, there were beautiful valleys there. She stopped.

"William."

"Ma'am."

She had me sit, then, and reached out with her eyes to hold my own. "Corn starch," she said, her hand to her chest. It was warm in this classroom, she said, it was always warm, and, like anyone in such a place, she would sweat. I might not have noticed, but she had breasts, she said, smiling, to support which she wore a bra. Heaviness and heat, more heat. She sprinkled corn starch in her bra, she said, and on her skin. It absorbed sweat, she said. It helped her stay cool, she said, and she needed all the help she could get to stay cool right now, and, she said, she enjoyed talking to me, after class or out by the track, to talk to someone curious and sensitive, but it was impolite to stare. Okay? Good boy.

Let it further be postulated that any line extends beyond its endpoints into infinity.

As to lines, say that though one is to connect two points, infinite combinations of lines other than the straight one might be drawn. I rode the side streets waywardly toward home, no need to hurry, my Uncle Earl and Aunt Sue were due in for a weekend's visit. Riding, with no traffic, as fast as I liked, weaving from curb to curb, pedaling with hands at my sides, the breeze on my face a long-delayed kiss, the only kiss I had yet known, my skin aching for the pressure, the touch or slightest brush, of feminine lips, houses dull blurs in the corners of my eyes and the naked boughs of trees impotently clawing as I blew by the brown yards, even in this ecstasy my cyclist's eye on the surface of the street. A broken patch of pavement, unseen rock, a slick of mud, even, will throw the tires from true, throw rider over handlebars. Attention goes, too, to any other moving object, lines tending to intersect and intersections posing, always, dangers, the riderly mind buzzing, therefore, with quick, unconscious calculations of velocity and vector. All of which is to say I saw the squirrel. That was not the problem. The problem was that the squirrel, squirrel-like, started to dart across my path, froze, reversed, and froze again. Having encountered this before, it being impossible to ride all over a squirrel-infested town, and what town isn't, without encountering the squirrel's stuttering progress, I was onto it, speeding but ready to swerve. The problem was a matter of intersecting lines, this particular squirrel on this particular occasion choosing, if choice governs in a brain so small, to reverse again and dash again right into my path, nothing for it then but to ride over with a crunch of tire on squirrelly spine. A wobble, a near loss of control, and I skidded to a stop and looked back. A mistake. I should have ridden on after having ridden over, the squirrel not yet dead, but clearly dying, back legs scrabbling, claws audible as they scratched at the pavement, straining to raise its head but held down, some invisible bully pinning its shoulders to the street with a giant thumb, if but some vengeful thumb pressed from above, if the divine thumbed at a thing so. All I could think of was the squirrels Earl shot for stew when we visited in Oklahoma, how they tumbled to sudden stops when the pellets struck and Earl quickly skinned them, yanking off the heads and tossing them with a scant handful of guts to the dogs chained up and waiting by the rusted-out old Ford, the butt and barrel of his cigarette fingerprinted in squirrel blood, and that maybe I was supposed to go finish the thing off, smash the skull with a loose chunk of curb, rather than let it lie there, in no hurry, it seemed, to be done on its own.

Over any point an infinite number of lines might be drawn. I shouldn't have worried. A car turned onto the street right then and, as I scooted my bike out of the way, finished the job, turning the squirrel inside out to leave a red and matted mess behind.

Saturday was a double feature. Triple if you counted the developing drama, mostly offstage, between my parents, the visiting aunt and uncle idly smoking around the kitchen table. The entertainment started with a film Earl and Sue showed us, laboriously setting up a screen in the living room while my father irritatedly raked around the yard, grumbling about the Pirates' Friday night loss and the indignity of visiting in-laws, calling us all to order, coffee cups refilled, Sue closing every curtain so the living room was orange-tinted dark and Earl firing up the projector. "A family home," said a deep voice, the picture showing a two-story house on a nice-looking street somewhere prettier than Centertown. But where was not? "A family in their home," the voice deep and assured in spite of the sprockets' sputter, family portrait of father and mother and boy and girl giving way to school photos and snapshots, suits and dresses, facing the camera, clowning in a yard, at a ballpark, beside a lake. "Christmas Eve, 1977," the voice said, and there were jingle bells ringing and stockings all hung by a chimney and a Christmas tree with lights, the camera zooming on the tree, on the lights, on one light, one bright yellow light that finally blurred the whole screen, the bells' sound drowned by flames and sirens, "a short-circuiting string of festive lights ignites the dry needles of the family tree, the one young Jim and Eleanor had helped to decorate just days before, and in an instant the tree was aflame. As the family slept, the fire spread quickly through the first floor, trapping them in rooms above." The screen darkened before a series of images, a charred black skeleton where the house had been, a stretcher with a sheet over whatever it carried. "In mere minutes, they were gone."

It turned out that all the poor family, all poor Jim and Eleanor and their mom and dad, had needed to save them from their fiery demise was a new line of smoke and fire detectors, battery-powered and independent of the home's electricity, which might be cut off during a fire, alarms whose klaxons were driven by a special gas canister, their noise sure to wake anyone within a city block, alarms triggered by special patented censors for heat and smoke, especially smoke because it was the smoke you had to worry about, most people were killed by it before they were ever touched by flames. The film slapped around its spool a few times until Earl switched off the projector and Sue opened the curtains, that poor family, what were they all going to get for Christmas before they burned up, and when Earl demonstrated the klaxon my father jumped and shouted "God damn." But even that was not the end because then Earl and Sue told us all about the company that made these new alarms.

"A good company," Earl said. "A real family operation. "And," Sue added, "a good Christian one." They had a picnic every summer for the folks who helped them save lives and spread the word, the boss, the very top guy of the whole thing, helping out at the grill and knowing everyone by name, so that it wasn't just luck that Earl got laid off and found his way into this family business, but it must have been the Lord himself.

"And since that moment when I met the man who has set out to save lives, the Lord has put a burden on my heart to bring the word of these miraculous alarms, which could have saved the lives of those poor children on that Christmas morning," Earl said, and Sue said "Praise God," and Earl said "to everyone we can, from people who open their door to me back home to loved ones like y'all," and so we ended up with a whole house setup of brand new alarms, the house now safe from sudden fire and destruction.

It was my mother's idea to send me to my second movie of the day, to this week's climactic feature of the Reverend Alan's flame-flyered revival, a film about damnation and salvation, the bright orange paper under her windshield at Kroger's one day telling her it was the perfect cure for our culture's hauntings and demonic possessions and did I know that Fats Crandall had, in his record collection, albums by groups called things like Judas Priest and no wonder he had peed off the gym roof. This might save me, plus it would be good for me to get out of the house, and on that maybe she had a point, the electric tension having risen over the course of the afternoon so that in the static it was impossible to think. It would be so good for me that she drove me herself and dropped me off at First Baptist, waiting and watching until I went inside for the rapture.

Because that's what the movie was about, of course, like a thief in the night the culling of the faithful, a woman waking to her husband's electric razor rattling around the sink, the man holding the razor having disappeared mid-shave, so much steam or mirror fog, others all over the city up like puffs of smoke from their clothes and cars, this transformation slowly understood by the solid remainder as the salvation of the disappeared, everyone still draped in meat therefore unsaved, having dallied and piddled and not gotten around to getting right with God, and, by the transitive process of equality or something, damned, and, sure enough, things took a turn for the worse what with the antichrist showing up and his minions running everything, though how this was so different from the corridors of Payne or the streets of Centertown was not immediately or persuasively apparent. The metal folding chairs of the fellowship hall made me wish my own body less substantial, more vaporously saved, able at least to float above the seat, and the popcorn promised on the flame-orange flyers was stale, kernels flattening rather than breaking when bitten, sticking to my teeth so that I had to pry them away with my tongue, the other endangered youth around me seeming, though, to have no such problem and watching the movie as if their lives and souls depended on it, Reverend Alan and Hal Lindsey, famous author of *The Late, Great Planet Earth*, having told them that this was, in fact, the case. You only had to look around you to see how the prophecies in the Book of Revelation were coming true, the Whore of Babylon riding around on the Common Market, and if you believed this stuff then of course you were going to shun Halloween and sing "Amen" and wonder what Hell must be like. It had started with the stuttery, warbly movie about the family burned up on Christmas morning, maybe, my father moving all morning through dooms of irritation, my mother's shoulders slowly rising up the rigid column of her neck, all of us stuck in too, too solid flesh no matter how much Earl and Sue smoked at the kitchen table, though this was to date the failures of salvation too recently, the razor rattling in the sink, when that was only the outward and visible, things having been, behind the scenes, beneath the skin, somewhere just beyond somatic or semantic reach, fucked up already, whispered recriminations shattering like glass against the kitchen wall.

    Things went to Hell, then, the antichrist and minions getting pretty tough on people who wouldn't swear themselves over to him, and though little groups hid out and prayed together, they weren't escaping into vapor, and finally everybody was going to get the Mark of the Beast and if you didn't you were going to get executed, the good Christians in their hideouts saying well, that would save their souls at least, and so up to the scaffold the woman marched with some others of the tardy faithful, but then it was all a dream and she woke up wide-eyed and gasping, her neck saved, blinking away the antichrist. But what had woken her up, what was that awful sound coming from the bathroom, clattering and buzzing and, for the knot of true believers aching on the metal folding chairs of the First Baptist fellowship hall, familiar? The electric razor shaving away at the insubstantial, grinding its blades against the sink until the film flapped from the sprockets and the reel spun on bright light, the Reverend Alan stepping up to preach. The flyer had said nothing about preaching, but, finger in floppy Bible and feathered hair peaked and parted over the forehead, this was the end foretold and if we attended to the signs and portents it was clear the end was getting pretty nigh, time for every one of us to look to his or her immortal soul because soon, oh too soon, the time of tribulation would be upon us. There was some singing then about the resurrection and the life, but I just moved my lips because I didn't know the words.

My mother was a rapture casualty, nowhere to be seen when the evening ended. I waited, watching other kids get into cars, watching cars leaving the lot, watching Reverend Alan and Kramer's mother congratulate each other on some solid soul saving, and when there was still no sign of her I headed for home on foot, having been one acquainted with the route and the chilly evening feeling like the saving breath of saints, yards and streets melted to silver under a big moon, the whole town rendered precious now that I had it to myself, the last person on earth during those moments when no cars passed. Did that make me the antichrist? The seals were broken as I turned our corner. I heard them before I saw, and wasn't sure whether to hurry then or turn around and stay in the heaven I had come through, keep walking out beyond the farthest city lights and take this circus all the way to the border. The noise was familiar, to our neighbors as well as to me, the shouting of my parents a regular enough feature of the soundscape, but this had a rarer element, a hysterical pitch I hadn't heard before, and when I finally heard my mother scream I ran the last half-block to our yard.

Posit a tableau: aunt and uncle standing by their car at the end of the driveway, back door open on model smoke alarm and film projector and case of Coors all hastily thrown onto the seat, mother and father standing at opposite ends of yard, mother in her corner weeping and pointing and screaming, "Just go, go and don't come back." And in his corner father hunched and puffed, fists at belt and hackles raised, bellowing, "Not about to be thrown out of my own goddamned house." Moonlit, porch lit, lit, too, from the windows and front doors of houses beside and across from ours, stark and complex intersections of multiply cast shadows, one falling over my mother's face when she saw me standing at the curb, a stranger half-recognized in her rage, someone she had known once, had forgotten now out of the usual order of things.

"Oh, Will," she moaned, leaning on the wrought-iron fence by the porch step. Earl was starting to say that my father was throwing him and Sue out. My father was shouting that it was none of my goddamned business but that I'd better say goodbye to these people, my mother's people, because "Guess what, you might not be seeing them again for a long time," not if he had anything to say about it and he by goddamn did, my mother weeping at me one moment sorry for not picking me up and the next screeching back at my father to just go why didn't he just go until my father, after some bull-like huffing and hoofing at the hard lawn, charged across, fists balled up at the ends of his arms, intent on punching his brother-in-law, an intersection that I, not sure what I meant to do, interrupted with a short line segment of my own, stepping into his path and stopping there, stopping his movement through space, stopping, for a long second, time, a magical power I had before this moment never once suspected I had and the best use of which I did not have quite a chance to contemplate there in the middle of such complicated geometry. I was well beyond the axioms here. A little spit flew from my father's lips as he turned on me, as a car turned on our street and slowly drove parallel to the curb, a yellow Sunbird so slow in its progress that it had not yet passed when my father, opening his fists at the last second, shoved me hard, handprints bruising already on my chest. I landed hard on my butt, registering the Sunbird slowly passing, the dashed gaze of Nicole Rose as, from the passenger seat and through the open window, her inscrutable face stared. Her cigarette, as she flicked it toward the scene of everyday domestic drama, traced an arc, a tumbling spark brightened as if by breath on its way toward extinction on the curb.

10.

WELL, IF IT WAS THE END OF THE WORLD, who said I had to spend it holed up in my bedroom listening to records? I made a little fire and huddled over it, the stiff pages of the coverless *Playboy* cold company, their unseeing stares unsatisfying, but still I took them from the foot locker, willing an eye to move, to widen, to look back, willing a breast to rise and fall upon a breath. The pages of poetry flipped by the fire, the words useless, their thin skin carrying the touch of Mrs. Jansen's fingertips, the taste, maybe, of her tongue, the finger briefly, thoughtlessly licked as she turned to the one she wanted, the fact of her wanting woven through the onionskin like smoke, the book a totem, fetish, relic, enshrined beside the butt Nicole had flicked toward my yard in passing, Nicole had touched, tasted, breathed through and on, and I had seen, taken, kept, held, brought here, its reek a relic of its own in the pocket of my jacket. Some say the world will end in fire. I fed the flames by my footlocker altar, invoking incarnation, closing my eyes on the gray thicket, incanting inwardly and calling *come to me, to touch, to taste,* Nicole standing there, hands cradling breasts, thumbs stroking skin, calling come to me, Mrs. Jansen sitting, saying it's not snow, opening the buttons of her blouse, Mrs. Jansen coming to me, her blouse open, saying *come.* Some say ice, my fingers on the pages, on the fawn filter, in my pants, saying *come,* Nicole or Mrs. Jansen, Nicole Rose and Mrs. Jansen, *come, come,* and when it was over, cold fingers wiped on cold jeans and cold feet kicking dirt over the sticky spot, this is the way the world ends, this is the way the world ends.

II

II.

CRUMBLING THAT EVENING'S COOKIE ON THE BRICKS *outside his window, he thinks Doctor Seymour is on to something, because what, really, has driven this compulsion (he is all right with calling it a compulsion) to eliminate the rodent is a growing sense that Gabriel does indeed have something to tell him. Some unwelcome news resonates from the squirrel as it nibbles at the buttered, sugared oats, gleams in its dark eye when, from time to time, the squirrel looks up, looks in, through the open window, right at him, the two of them frozen there, a couple of feet apart, thrums in the gelid air between them. He could not say when he first realized, in an inchoate way, that the glance the squirrel shot at him, whether on its approach along the bough to his window or when encountered on a walk across campus or when glimpsed at work or play in the courtyard, was a knowing glance, but he has come to feel that nothing about his deepening acquaintance with the creature is an accident. This nightly feeding, baiting, is his attempt to steer things to the destination of his choosing, one in which the emanations almost visible around the animal as it stands up on the window ledge, black claws at rest before the crooked seam running down its chest, are stilled.*

The seam. At first, he thought it was just a normal pattern in the squirrel's fur, a part or cowlick, kind of, one of those places where, hair growing against hair, a fault line or flaw in the pelt occurred. Increasingly, as the squirrel stands for longer moments, closer, almost in the full light cast by the lamp on his desk, it seems to be a scar, the skin shining where it has closed and grown over what must have been a grievous injury, and that's no surprise, given the way Gabriel sneaks and steals and bullies around the courtyard. Squirrels must fight, he thinks, out of the sight of people and predators, and it might be that the way their corpses litter the street season after season is not because they fall from branches or the power lines on which they run, not because they blunder under the wheels of cars, but, instead, because they have run afoul of one another, gotten caught up in vendettas or the simpler violence of creatures driven and derided by scarcity.

Tonight, the little bastard seems subtly to gesture at the scar, as if to say it's earned its stripes, its pride of place, its crumbling cookie, and he wonders whether he has misnamed the squirrel, misidentified it in the angelic order, whether he's leaving sweet fragments for Azazel or Lucifer. Claws poised over the scar tonight as if prepared to zip it open again, the squirrel spilling its guts onto his organized, right-angled, perfectly aligned desk. They stare at each other, a new ritual before the homework can begin, stare until, starting to feel fear rising like black bile into his throat, he nudges a cookie fragment at the beast, startling it, sending it, for the moment, back onto its bough, from which it watches, waiting until late, after the lamp is switched off and he is lying unsleeping, it comes and takes what it has come to see as its own.

12.

HERE IS A CROWD IN THE COURTYARD, many are chanting, words and phrases hard to make out, what are the words, where do the phrases end and in their ends are their beginnings, chanting rhythmic and continuous, while others shout over, into, against the chanting. The crowd in the courtyard surges around the little open space into which the blindfolded ones are led. There is always a voice over the scene, translating sometimes the chanting, sometimes the shouting, sometimes simply saying what is being shown. How we got to this moment, this chanting and shouting in the courtyard, this leading and jostling of the blindfolded ones, the leading by ones with weapons, rifles slung over a shoulder or held across the chest. The ones who lead the blindfolded ones look impassive and neither chant nor shout and then one of the blindfolded ones stumbles. It is a brief moment. One stumbles and the one escorting quickly and as if casually, as if unconsciously, takes the stumbling one's arm and holds the stumbling one up.

The scene replays over and over and everywhere, on the evening news and during breaks when the networks air updates. It punctuates the new late-night half-hour of further coverage, a comma between where one phrase ends and in its ending is a beginning. Still photographs accompany the news in the week's papers and illustrate the covers of magazines, hatred seething and boiling around the space through which the lethal guides the vulnerable, a spectacle of violence and power, the hand involuntarily reaching to support the one who stumbles in the middle of it all, the chanting and shouting and jostling, the rifles carried across the chest.

In Centertown, there were several schools of thought, some saying go right now and rain down bombs and send in troops, go now and get our people out and set those mullahs straight, an invasion just the thing though nobody had heard of this country the year before, just the thing to free the hostages and while we're at it show those Russians that we were a nation not to mess with, just the thing to teach our youth sacrifice and discipline and proper values and respect for their country and its tradition, nothing so forming the citizen as service abroad in his nation's armed forces, while others worried that such a response, however desirable in its immediate consequence—the destruction of a population chanting Death to America in its city's streets—and in the salutary effects it might have on the home front, would have additional and unintended consequences, would, maybe, draw into the conflict just those Russians against whom we had pushed and pulled and subtly, coldly fought for thirty years. No sense heating up the Cold War like that, so, three, send in a crack team of commandos, first mission to liberate the hostages but, second, wipe out some of those bearded, beady-eyed sonsabitches stirring up the student radicals, there being, after all, ways to cover our tracks, and just look at what the Israelis had managed at Entebbe, for instance, now *that* was a country that knew how to get things done on the ground, though, four, feeding the flames under that cauldron might be just the thing, these events being, as was obvious to anyone familiar with the texts, signs of the impending apocalypse, Ayatollah and Antichrist one and the same, some seeing in Persia portents and sensing with dread their significance, others, on the same evidence, applauding and packing their spiritual bags.

Was I the only one who saw in the moment assurance of an unconscious ethic of care, a subtle gesture of assistance most important because least intended? Newscasters emphasized the history, the politics, everyone a sudden expert on Iran, the Shah, the Ayatollah, and the student-led rebellion that had captured the embassy. My parents and classmates focused on the hate and turned hate back upon the scene, hate stuck on bumpers all over town, Mickey Mouse raising a white-gloved middle finger. I could not look away, watched the footage every time it ran, and it ran all the time, and, sure, the tiny moment was just an example of instinct, the gesture not a considered response, but that just meant that our instinct was for tenderness.

On TV, everything had changed. In Centertown, there were just new bumper stickers and the odd yellow ribbon on a tree, and after the late-night rerunning of the footage, the routine acquaintance with the streetlight scene, me trying to outwalk the furthest city light but finally palely loitering in the shadow of Nicole Rose's mimosa, and it was as I concluded yet another vigil there, staring at the front door from which Nicole did not emerge and at the side window from which no light shone, giving up and planning to go home, that the figure emerged from the shadows of oaks in another yard and I was caught.

The figure stood between me and the corner, blocking one way but leaving the dead-end to the park, through which I could maybe walk as if I had been doing nothing wrong, as if it were bright noontime, this apparition emerging from beneath the boughs left to mind its own business, and so I started that way, feeling, as I walked, the shadow stalking after me, hearing footsteps not my own on the carpet of fallen leaves. I waited for the voice to fall, a club between my shoulder blades, but it came only as I crossed the creek to go into the park, surprisingly not the voice of a man protecting his neighborhood from Peeping Toms but of a girl saying, "Please wait." When I started up the park side of the creek bank, the shadow behind me slipping audibly and falling back toward the trickle in the bed, saying again "Wait, stop." I turned to see a hooded sweatshirt, *Corpus Christi* in cursive across the front, and in it, when she pulled the hood down, Nicole Rose.

"Don't run off," she said, wiping her hands on her jeans. "I don't want to get all muddy chasing you."

She picked her way across the creek bed and was closer to me now than she had ever been, close so that I could smell the spring grass in her shampoo, smell her cinnamon chewing gum. "Are you going to help me up this or what?" I offered my hand and only when I had pulled her up the bank and when we both had let go did it occur to me that I had just held Nicole Rose's hand, but then she was walking away from me, walking to the swing set, where she sat on a swing and said it turned out I wasn't the only one who could do this spying on people thing, her dark eyes on my face as I stared at the silver shimmer of the grass in the moonlight and the deep dark of the trees around the park. You wake and wait and lie in bait.

"Busted," she said.

"I'm not a Peeping Tom," I said.

Well okay then what was I, she wondered, pushing herself back in the swing and twisting to one side until the chains kissed, then twisting back the other way, then turning to face me straight on again.

"I can't sleep," I said, and she let the swing come to a rest and nodded. The moon a half-open eye above, the park below perhaps an eye lashed by the trees around it, staring back. Nicole's eyes were on me now, her stare steady, here there was no place that did not see. I felt, under all of these eyes, caught, revealed, penetrated, but it was strangely not unpleasant this sensation, though scary, though maybe she was scared herself. Who knew what was going on behind those eyes, anger, disdain, curiosity? Yes, she certainly seemed curious.

"I wanted to help," I said, knowing the truth of this only as I said it.

Nicole pushing away my wanting as she pushed herself from the swing and walked across the silver grass, casting no shadow in the strange light, maybe a ghost, maybe not Nicole at all, an apparition on its way to disappearing in the shadows, until she turned toward me, turned solid again, asking did I ever come here, to the park, when I got tired of spying, saying she had come through this park a thousand times but never like this. "It's like a negative, you know? The sky is dark and the grass is bright. Everything's opposite." Her voice a voice I had not heard for all my standing and staring, deeper and softer than I had expected, opening a way, letting me closer. "What you saw," she said, turning to fix me in place with a look. "That night. If you tell anyone, Hector will kill you."

We were standing now beside the playground's centerpiece, a tall tower, four levels enclosed by steel bars, four chambers through which kids climbed all the way to the top, to the view over trees and all around Centertown, the shops, the stadium and school, the weapons plant, a long aluminum slide depending from an opening on the third floor, the slanted sheet glowing now, coldly molten. Something slipped, behind Nicole's mask or in the sudden stiff static between us, shifted and we were not strangers.

"You can't sleep," she was saying, "so you just walk around?"

When I said it was a different world at night, nobody to see you, when I said you could go anywhere, see all sorts of things nobody saw because nobody looked, when I asked whether she ever did the same, she shook her head and said it was different for girls. Feeling the wanting to help and the wanting not wanted, I found the gift I could offer.

"Can I show you something?"

"It's not your dick, is it?"

She took the hand I offered, and I made sure to say to myself now that I was holding Nicole Rose's hand. She followed me through the park and up Harvard Street. I left her at the curb in front of my house just long enough to wheel my newly repaired bike from its place beside the garage. It was awkward, at first, Nicole on the seat and me standing on the pedals, the bike wobbly as we approached the corner, but her hands held my waist and the bike picked up speed and soon we were out of the neighborhood and zig-zagging through back streets, down the alley behind strips of shops, across Centertown Road and through the Baptist parking lot. I never having to say hold on as we sped down the hill from Pleasant View or to lean with me as we rounded the Pipeline curve, never saying anything, either of us, no need, the gift given and accepted. At the edge of the brightly lit lot of the new Target, I stopped and Nicole watched as I slalomed around the standards, saying "Your turn" when I had ridden across the lot and back.

"Time me," she said, and why, how, had I never imagined that she would, that she could, even, ride like this, pedaling hard before swerving this way and that, dangerously close to the yellow columns from which the lights grew like beanstalks, her hair flying behind her as she flew, crouched over handlebars and leaning into turns? As she rode back toward me, standing to pump the pedals on the last straightaway, she grinned, a little girl who had, of course, it hit me now, once been, incomprehensively, inconceivably, impossibly, a little girl laughing, crying, smiling, raging, by turns cute and annoying, time past and time present both present in her breathless braking smile. I stared exaggeratedly at my wristwatch.

"Not bad," I said. "For a rookie."

And it was on, turns taken in the race around the parking lot, times compared, and when I asked, after a couple of rounds, if she was winded, worried she would say yes, she'd had enough, she said yes but asked if we could ride some more. "Of course," I said. "Hop on, I'll drive." She perched on the handlebars now and though this made it hard to see, to steer, though it made our progress slow and uncertain, I thrilled at her hair in my face, the fragrance of her hooded sweatshirt, of her hair and skin, soap, sweat, the faint whiff of smoke. I could have ridden thus behind her all night long, but hard as I pedaled in any other direction the neighborhood began to pull us back and I was surprised when the irresistible gravity brought us finally to the park from which we had, seconds ago, it seemed, departed hand in hand from a world full only of weeping. I coasted to the tower, stopping in the deep sand by the foot of the slide.

"That was amazing," Nicole said, sliding from the handlebars, her face close, her eyes holding mine. "You do that all the time?"

"Sometimes, when I can't sleep."

"When you're not looking through my window," her hand lifting mine now from the handlebar, her fingers curling under mine and squeezing, eyes and hands now interlocked. I did not need to worry. I was, if I must be, forgiven. "But," she said, "don't spy on me," whispering, and I whispered "Okay," and instead, she said, "bring me with you," and "Okay," I said and before I could wonder whether or when, our lips were pressed against each other, Nicole's tongue flickering quickly against mine, and before I could say to myself that we were kissing, I was kissing Nicole Rose, or, better, being kissed by her, kissing, she was smiling, whispering good night, and I stood astride my bike watching her walk toward the trees, waved back when she turned to wave, and only when she was so completely gone that I could doubt she had been there to begin with, turned around to slowly pedal home.

13.

ANDY, THE WAREHOUSE MANAGER, SANG "Wasted Days and Wasted Nights" along with Freddy Fender and broke down some cardboard boxes while I pushed a broom around pallets of copy paper and file folders. There was not much work to do, the trucks having come and been unloaded, the orders having all been filled and shipped, while I was following Mrs. Jansen's unenthusiastic lead through *Romeo and Juliet,* about which the best thing she could say, she had said, was that at least Shakespeare also thought the young lovers were stupid, and we would all be best off if we listened to Mercutio, *a pox on both your houses,* or, if we couldn't do that, then take to heart the line where Juliet suggests that she and Romeo just hold hands.

"She should have taken her own advice, Juliet, it would have saved her life and everyone else some heartache, because, and this is what people miss in the play," Mrs. Jansen said. "Desire running amok wrecks everything. Young love. Remember, kids, that boy came to the party looking for one girl and ended up falling for another, the worst one he could fall for." She rubbed her fingertips along the dark half circles under her eyes. We didn't want to believe a word that boy said, she urged us.

"I've got," Andy said, "a coupla pornos you can look at if you want."

I made a few bucks working in the warehouse, usually on weekends, usually when things were busy or Andy was shorthanded, but today I was only killing time until my father was finished. My mother had left for a visit with Aunt Sue, needing, she had said, some time to think things over. I would rather have biked or even walked to or from school, but those possibilities had been washed out by rain driving down out of the steel-wool sky, as my father put it, as if something up there had sprung a leak, as if a cow were pissing on a rock. Rain had battered Centertown all day, beaten the town like that was its job, knocking the last leaves off of every tree, the soaked clutter clogging storm drains and backing water up in yellow-brown puddles along the sides of every street. Something up there wanted to wash us all away, it seemed, or at least, an errant drop finding its way around every opened umbrella or raised collar to trace its chilly course down the back of the neck, to insult each of us with a jet of cold spit from above. The rain had stopped now, but the gutters still ran and every pothole was a puddle. I was messing around with the pallet jack, standing on the blades and pumping the handle to lift myself a couple of feet off the ground, pressing the release lever to ride back to earth.

"Couple hundred, more like," I said, and Andy said he'd gotten some new ones, one with the world's biggest titties in it, honest to God you couldn't tell how the poor girl could stand up. "And be careful on that jack," he said. "You don't want to end up with your old man's toes. That'd put an end to your track star career."

I had never heard exactly how my father's toes had come to be so wrecked. An accident. That was the most anyone had said. When I was a baby. Something had crushed them somehow, left him with the twisted tragedies that brought him, every few months, back to the podiatrist, that left him, always, walking gingerly in the hard-soled shoes he had to wear for work.

"How did my dad hurt his toes?" I said.

"Fucking around with a pallet jack," Andy said, and when he saw that I thought he was joking, he said "No, really. Or maybe someone else was messing with it. Pasco told me, long time ago, but he didn't know all the details. Your dad was in the service. One way or another, pallet full of something awful—guns or bombs or Agent fucking Orange—got dropped and crushed his every last toe." Andy turned a page and whistled, held it up for me to see. He was right. It was hard to figure how the pneumatically endowed blonde kept her balance. "He was lucky it only dropped from a few inches. Farther and that pallet might have crushed his toes clean off. As it was, from what Pasco said, the docs thought about cutting them all off."

"Jesus," I said.

"Saved his bacon, though," Andy said. "Ain't no way you can ship out to the 'Nam with ten crushed piggies. Your dad got a medical discharge and came to work for P&C. Wish to fuck I'd've got my toes crunched up."

With no work to be done and with the skies having, for the moment, closed back up, content, for now, to glower and threaten, I said goodbye to Andy and changed into my shorts and running shoes. My father had said it was fine to get my road work in by running home from the warehouse if the rain stopped, but I should not come crying to him if I got run over on the highway, and by the way would it kill me to clean up the kitchen when I got to the house. There were neither side roads nor sidewalks along this stretch of the old highway, and though I had run it before it was not made for running, the shoulder littered with broken glass, the sides of the two-lane lined with anonymous, low-slung concrete rectangles that made or stored, processed or sold I could not tell what. Centertown's first bars were here, the T-Bird and the Yellow Jacket, dives whose old neon signs still flickered in the deepening dusk and in whose parking lots the pickups of dedicated drunks slowly rusted. A couple of motels punctuated the miles of warehouses, one as old as the defense plant, a two-story Oasis whose rooms rented by the hour or by the week, its own bar now defunct, the O'Aces playing card sign still visible beside its boarded-over door, and a new motel, opened when the new entry ramp linked the old highway with the airport freeway, one with no bar but cheek by jowl with B.G.'s Country Kitchen so that travelers could get eggs and coffee without having to drive all the way to civilization. A red splotch in its parking lot, spied out of the corner of my eye as I passed, resolved itself at the last second into Dr. Paul Stark's red Ferrari. I slowed and stopped and looked again and sure enough, complete with the doctor's patented diagonal-across-two-spaces parking job, the unmistakable feral machine rested, a single gout vivid against the washed out fence and pavement, against the gravel colored air, a subliminal flicker for drivers passing at fifty miles per, an attractive hazard for me as I passed, and stopped, on foot. The red drew me, a warming, warning, flame, my jog into the parking lot casual, as if this were part of my customary route. It rested, coiled, perhaps, to spring, as, no one else around to see, I reached, waiting for my hand to scorch, and touched the finish.

Cold metal, as inert against my skin as the finish was fiery to the eye.

It was pathetic, sure, but there was something in the icy trickle that navigated the umbrella, evaded capture, and invaded the gap between collar and neck, that coursed its cold way over the skin, down the spine, leaving in its wake a shiver and a sudden, panicked flock of goose bumps, that felt personal. Aimed and intended, it had to be, for what were the chances, and it would, maybe, have been better for some vengeful sprite to steer that soul-dampening drop on its way, better than the thought, standing in wet shoes and socks and sweaty T-shirt, that none of it had anything to do with me, it was just the cold, wet way of the world. Mrs. Jansen's tan raincoat neatly folded in the passenger seat of the red car, however it left me to prune and shrivel, was not an insult, though my guts shuddered and shrank against its injury. The car was Stark's. The car was at the motel. Stark was in the motel. The coat was hers, here, in the car, so she was here, in the motel, with Stark.

And hadn't I known? Well, there was knowing and there was knowing, a deep, junk-littered and weed-choked ravine between the unacknowledged understanding, seeing Mrs. Jansen and her college chum standing beside the car in one or another parking lot, and the ocular proof, raincoat on car seat, of teacher and lover, the word a gut punch, sneaking off to the edge-of-town darkness of corporate anonymity. There was knowing and there was, now, fresh from Andy's porn collection, knowing the positions and permutations, imagining all too well, in full and fleshy detail, all the intertwined limbs and sucking mouths, all the rubbings and tuggings, the blissful rictuses, and somewhere in all this knowing lurked the lonely impulse of despair.

In the courtyard, one, blindfolded, stumbled, and another, without thinking, stepped and reached out, caught the arm and held it.

It was with something like surprise that I found myself trying the glass door at the back of the motel, the one, surely, through which Stark had led Mrs. Jansen, out of view of the highway. When it turned out to be locked, I pounded with my open hand as if I hoped to smash into the anteroom I could see there, the blue-lit chamber, undisturbed ice machine, soda machine, cigarette machine reflecting back my impotence, my impotence inspiring the laughter of that garish carpet on the stairs. Whether summoned by my knocking or just passing on her rounds, the motel housekeeper appeared and asked in Spanish if señor had lost his key, suggested in Spanish that I could go around to the front desk to get another.

"*Por favor,*" I shouted, slapping at the glass. "*Por favor,*" something—my thinly breaking voice, my pathetic pawing—persuading the housekeeper to push the bar, release the lock, and, as I slipped inside, gesture toward the motel's mouth and say again that I could go to the front desk.

"*Gracias,*" I said, shouldering past her, into the hallway and around her cart full of towels and tiny bars of soap. But what, now that I was inside? Lined up on either side of the turquoise carpet, closed doors stared blankly at each other, ignoring the interloper, offering no clue as to what, who, was behind. Should I knock on each in turn? And what if the sneaky couple were on the second floor? Not knowing, I walked down the hallway, not noticing the numbers as they counted down, not thinking of how I might explain myself to the desk clerk, not imagining what I might say when I found them. A whiff of smoke arrested me and I turned and sniffed and tracked it back to a door in front of which I stood for a long moment, sure, somehow, it was the right one. I knocked. The silence, in reply, deepened, solidified into a presence, a shadow on the other side, leaning and listening. The housekeeper had wheeled her cart along the hallway and now she stopped nearby and watched me knock again, harder, the silence shifting on the other side, thickening to a murmur, a movement, a step toward the door.

"Mrs. Jansen," a croak through my closed throat. "Are you in there?"

Rustling now, the silence shattered and dropped in shards on the awful carpet, whispering, the housekeeper backing away as if she could hear it, as if she feared what might, when the door finally opened, peek out or emerge. Stark's shirt was only halfway buttoned and his hair was messed up. He held the door partway opened and stared wordlessly at me. The smoke smell was stronger now and I could hear another body moving in the room.

"What can I do for you, son?"

"Mrs. Jansen?" I whispered.

"She's gonna need another minute, okay?"

The door closed and, as if assured that all was well, the housekeeper wheeled her cart on down the hall, bringing the reestablishment of order to room after room, reserving her power for that later moment when she would return to this one, would clean up the traces, replace the sheets, set everything to right. But, before that, there was this moment, the doctor opening the door again, holding it wide, bowing and gesturing to me like a footman, presenting, ta-da, Mrs. Jansen standing by the window, her blouse misbuttoned so that it hung crookedly from her shoulder. No housekeeper was ever going to get things back to normal here. Smoke rose still from the half-stubbed cigarette in the ashtray, from Mrs. Jansen's lips the acrid sound of my name.

"William?"

Everything sharp was blurry now in the weak light fighting through the window and the sheer drape. Mrs. Jansen held a Camel pack, turned it over in her hands. "What are you doing here?"

Oh, you know, out for a run, in the neighborhood, and, say, see, what a coincidence. Out for a run, almost ran right by. Out for a run and caught, tripped up and tangled, by the sight, red blur in the corner of the eye, punch and blood spot on the periphery. Running and arrested by the sight. The car. Red car. A stumble in the courtyard, an instinctive step out of the road, hand out for the errant elbow. "His car," and "I see," she said. "Sit down, William. We need to talk."

"Nothing good ever follows that sentence, kid," the doctor said.

"Paul," Mrs. Jansen said. "Can you give us a few minutes?"

Stark said sure, he would go get sodas, did I want one, and when he had gone and closed the door behind him, Mrs. Jansen pointed to the armchair in the corner of the room. I sat. Mrs. Jansen took the end of the hastily made bed, turning the cigarette pack over and then over again, her hair disheveled and the skin of her neck and the part of her chest revealed by the misbuttoned blouse as splotchy and red as her face was pale. When I said I was there to help her, her chest laughed and her face cried at the same time and her fingertips were cool on my cheek.

"I've messed up, William."

I looked at the rumpled covers on the bed. She smiled. "Well, maybe that way too." Smoothed the bedspread around her. Definitely that way, too, and she couldn't imagine what I must think of her, but what she meant, what she needed to talk about with me, was that she had messed up not by messing around with Paul Stark but by making a mistake with me. How old did I think she was? You weren't supposed to ask a woman her age, or to tell her what you thought it was. I did not know much about talking with women, but I knew that much, though I could not say how. TV probably. But Mrs. Jansen didn't need me to answer. She was thirty, she said, thirty, and god it sounded old sometimes but it also seemed so young, it seemed she had just graduated, had just started out, it seemed she had so many things to try still, things to do, she hadn't been outside this country ever except for once to Mexico, in college, on Spring Break, and that hardly counted, there was the whole world still to explore. You thought you were so young and there was all this time, but then, thirty, you were settled in Centertown, how had that happened, and married to the local hero who had grown up to be a pillar of the community, but you know what pillars did, they stood in place and held things up and maybe things could be tied to them, but they did not go anywhere, how could they, they were pillars, and if you were tied to a pillar, well then you weren't going anywhere either.

"Thirty, William, and starting to feel stuck here." And here was the kind of place where if you felt stuck there wasn't a whole lot to make it better. She had loved so many things in college, books and movies and music, and what was there here to feed that kind of appetite. Well, she knew, she could tell from the first day I walked into her classroom, I was a kindred spirit, the way I had soaked up whatever she had suggested, the way I sat in that rapt way, grabbing up whatever pearl she might toss into the trough, so little here for someone like me, someone like her. Settled down in Centertown and sometimes, some nights when Bo was staying at the station, she could not sleep and she stood outside on their quiet block near the library and the night would be stifling and she felt she could not breathe, and on the nights her husband spent at home, she could not even go outside and let the weight lift off her chest and up into the orange light of the suburban night, but lay there with it crushing her instead and wondered what she had done, how she had, without seeing it coming, ended up here.

But it wasn't my job to do anything about that.

"I have been one acquainted with the night," I said. I went out late, too, walking all over town, riding, now that my bike was fixed. I knew what she meant.

I knew something, yes, she said, but I could not know yet what it was to feel yourself turn thirty here, could never know what it was to be the woman, the prize brought home to Centertown by Bo, the hero, to be yoked to freshman English and the Payne High Pirates, to be stuck selling concessions on a Friday night, smoking in silence as the town contemplated burning its youth, to be smothered just as she felt she was waking up because she was the wife, the role model, and god I could not yet know what it was to want in the long nights. (Oh but couldn't I? Hadn't I lain for hours in my own room, my skin burning to be touched, on fire until I could pedal or walk the heat from it?)

And then Stark had shown up, Paul, melting chains and shackles in the acid of his disregard, and oh yes there was plenty to say about how complicated this all was, she was up all night now not with that simple, so simple now she missed it, sense of stifling but, instead, for better and worse, aflame at once with need and guilt, I could not imagine, she had not been able, before, to imagine, the guilt, the way it fell as if the leaden sky had been let go to drop on her, and I could not imagine how, even under all that, the flame kept licking and tickling and burning through her resolve and here she was.

"Once, down at the Gulf," she said, "I saw a dead gull that kept getting caught up by the waves. It would wash up on the sand and then another wave would come along and tumble it around, this poor gull, all ragged and gray and just tumbling in the foam and rubbing against the sand until the waves left it alone for a minute."

But that wasn't what she meant to say, she interrupted herself. This wasn't what she needed me to understand. The mess she was making with Paul was one thing, but that was her thing, she would deal with it. This mess, though, her and me, this was one we had to deal with together, because she hadn't realized, oh sure, it was nice to be the object of a student crush, it was an occupational hazard, and it was new to her to be singled out by someone so sensitive, so bright. But she was my teacher, she was, young as she felt, so much older, or, to put it the other way, I was, however I might chafe at it, so much younger ("Oh, William, so young"), I had no idea, and she had known, you could *not* not know, watching my eyes, and instead of dousing that had, she knew, let herself flirt and feed the flames, flames she knew all too well, and now here I was and what did I think there was between us, what could there ever possibly be between us?

"My mother is gone," I said. "My parents had a big fight and she left."

Her fingertips touched my face. I could not know it now, she told me, but I was going to be so much more than fine. It was hard now, hard to know how short this part of my life was, how, if I could just get away from here, all that went wonderfully for me would leave this time as just a shadow. There would be college and books and music and movies. There would be Rilke and Godard. But she was stuck here, she was going to have to make do. I didn't have to help her, she would be okay. I shouldn't worry about her, shouldn't think about her, even, beyond the homework she was still going to make me do. I should send her a postcard sometime.

"You don't have to be stuck," I said, and when she said that Stark was not someone you ran away with, that if she were available he would lose interest, he would not have been so hot to get her into rooms like this if she had been free, I said, "Not him. Not the doctor." This was how I could help. We could go, we could take this circus all the way to the border. I had, of course, never been to Mexico.

She smiled and touched my face again and didn't I know that even Springsteen didn't like that song? There was a knock at the door and then the doctor was back, sipping a Coke and offering the can to Mrs. Jansen.

"We should give him a ride," she said.

"It's okay," I said. "I was running. I can run the rest of the way."

"He's running," the doctor said.

"We should give him a ride," Mrs. Jansen said.

The Ferrari had only two seats, the doctor said, but that was fine, the teacher said, it would give her time to straighten up. The doctor shrugged and took a towel from the bathroom, tossing it to me and saying, "Sit on that." When we were in the car and Stark started it up, the engine purred, sleek and satisfied, the big cat having hunted, having eaten its fill. It moved quickly when the doctor put it into gear, though, and I could hear the lingering hunger in the engine because it wanted, always, to run faster. As we idled, waiting to turn out onto the highway, I could hear how barely controlled it was as the doctor held it with the brake and the clutch, and when an opening came and the doctor released the car, I could feel its joy at leaping into the lane and straightening and speeding smoothly right up to the car ahead and sliding into the other lane to pass, and running ahead, happy to be running and not hunting, these cars were not its prey. At the intersection, the Ferrari dove right instead of left, veered away from my neighborhood and kept on the rightward bend onto Trinity, even as I was saying we missed the turn to my house, it was back there, that way.

"You want to drive this baby or not?" the doctor said.

When we had passed the back of the plant and were on the road through the river bottoms, the doctor pulled over and idled on the shoulder. "Ever drive a stick?"

"I've driven my uncle's truck a couple of times," I said, "out in the country."

"This isn't your uncle's truck," the doctor said when we had traded places. He showed me how to release the brake, to put the car in gear. I lifted my foot from the clutch and touched the gas, the car jumping and bucking and dying in the gravel. Not my uncle's truck, Stark said again, but a sensitive and specialized piece of driving technology.

"You don't have to choke it or grind it or anything. Just let it feel what you want to do."

After a couple of tries, I got it moving and I understood what Stark meant. The slightest touch of the gas, tiniest turn of the wheel, and the car intuited my wish, the speedometer's needle lifting on the straightaway though I did not urge it on. Out here was where Hector Rose and his friends raced, their girlfriends gathering at the wide shoulder to watch, and here I was, behind the wheel of a red Ferrari, slowing as we came up to the S-curve, the doctor saying, "Don't hold her back, just pick a line and go." I tapped the gas and gripped the wheel as the engine roared and the car jumped into the curve, hugging the pavement and sending through its struts and through my feet and spine and hands its hot desire to shoot through and streak a blur of red against the high yellow-gray grass of the Bottoms, but how did you steer through a double curve at such speed, and what happened if you missed, if you took the wrong line? I lifted my foot from the pedal but the car still thrummed and sped. I touched the brake, the car and the doctor both sighing in disappointment. I tried to speed up again, but I'd forgotten to shift down and the car chugged accusingly and "Here," the doctor said when we had crossed the narrow bridge and the road widened again, "pull over here."

At the front of the Ferrari, I stood, holding the towel now damp from my shorts and shirt, the air around us damp, clinging to my shirt and skin, weighing down the grass, the gray sky itself sagging, washed out, wrung out, the doctor saying don't sweat it.

"Karen says you're a smart kid. Are you?"

"Smart enough," the doctor said when I kept staring at the tall grass, taller than the two of us. We could, one or the other or both, disappear out here in this tall grass, a car run off the road and into the curtain that would close behind us. Smart enough to know that fourteen was less than half of thirty, that there were things you had to be old enough for, had to be ready for. Some things would be great when the time was right. When the time was right, I'd find myself driving a beautiful machine right through the curves and everything would feel good and go just as fast as it all wanted to go, and this was probably, I thought, a talk my father was supposed to have with me but here I was standing in front of the car, which rumbled quietly, relaxed but ready to spring.

"But there are things," Stark went on, "adult things, you just might not be ready for and if you tried them before you were ready, before you knew how they worked, before you could feel how things wanted to go and you could relax and focus at the same time and let them go, you'd fuck things up."

Did I get him? See where he was going with this?

"You could really fuck things up, my friend."

Mrs. Jansen leaning tiredly against her desk at the front of her classroom, looking anxiously around the parking lot as she walked toward the red car after school, sitting on the edge of the motel room bed with her elbows on her knees, the cigarette smoldering on the nightstand behind her.

"You're not making her happy," I said, and the doctor smiled, looking off down the Bottoms road toward where it bent to Arlington, looking off at the grass curtain alongside the road. We could, one or the other or both, disappear down here and it might take months, it had in the past sometimes taken months when someone disappeared down here, to find them.

"Yeah," the doctor said, "well, sometimes it's not about happy."

He started toward the driver's side door, and as I went toward the passenger side, the doctor put his hand on my shoulder, saying "You like her, I get that," his fingers squeezing at the point where my arm joined my shoulder, finding a little bundle of nerves there, squeezing hard, a paralyzing pain shooting down my arm. But I should never again pull a stunt like this one today. "Get it?" The fingers squeezed harder for a second, tears welling in my eyes, my shoulder pinned as if to the pavement by a hand from above.

"Get in," the doctor said, letting go and tapping my shoulder. "I'll take you home."

"I'll walk," I said.

The doctor looked at me for a minute, his lips pressed into a tight, white line, and then he shrugged. "Fuck it," he said. "You want to walk, walk."

He slid into the car and even as the door shut, the beast was coiling to spring. In a roar and squeal and blur of red, the car pulled a U-turn on the crumbling blacktop, sped by me, and was gone.

It took me until after eight to get home, the darkness dropping quickly, and I wished I had brought my sweatshirt. I was shivering and hungry, and I knew as I opened the front door that something was not right. There were no lights on in the house, but that was no problem. Over time, I had learned to navigate the front hallway in total darkness. I could do it with my eyes closed. I could see the shapes of things: the little table on which my mother had put a vase of fake flowers and where we all dropped our keys as we came in, the rickety coat rack my father had picked up for fifty cents at a yard sale, even the shape of the woven rug on which no one ever wiped their feet. There were no smells of cooking, and I wondered if my father had waited, thinking that I would make us dinner. Or maybe he had eaten out. A glow came from the living room, which meant that the television was on, which meant that my father was there to watch it. I took a deep breath and walked out of the dark hallway.

"Nice run?" my father said.

He was stretched out on the couch in his work suit, a glass balanced on his stomach. A black and white movie was on, the volume low.

"I ran into someone," I said. "Fats. I figured it would be okay if I walked around with him for a while."

"You eat?" he said. I said we had gotten burgers at the Dairy Queen near Fats's house. He nodded and shifted, sliding his legs out of the way, and gestured toward the end of the couch with his head. "Come on," he said. "Movie's only been on for a few minutes. Join me."

When I started to sit, he stopped me. "Wait," he said. He held up the glass. "Grab me some more ice, will you? And get a glass for you, too."

I filled his glass and another one with ice. He poured an inch into each glass from the bottle on the floor.

"Cheers."

It didn't seem as if I had a choice. My father had never offered me a drink before, and his offer now bore with it an assumption that I would accept. I sipped. The whiskey, cold in my mouth from the ice, grew warmer as it traveled down my throat, and bloomed into orange warmth in my chest. I suppressed an urge to cough, but I could tell that my father sensed it anyway. He smiled.

"This movie," he said. "It's a great one. *Battleground.* Classic war flick."

We watched for a while without talking, and though I had missed the first few minutes it was easy to catch up. The movie focused on a squad of infantrymen stuck in the Battle of the Bulge. One guy, Holley, had returned to the unit after recovering from a wound. He would say, once in a while, when the platoon had to dig in yet again after moving from one place to another, "I found a *home* in the Army." My father chuckled at that.

"I felt exactly the same way," he said. "Best time of my life, the service."

He had never talked much about his time in the Army. I knew that he had served, but he had never been in combat, never been farther away than Fort Hood, where he had gone for basic training. This was all when I was a baby. It didn't come up much. He'd managed not to go to Vietnam, but I could never tell, when he did say anything about it, or when he pointedly said nothing about it, whether that was a good thing or not.

"This one kid," he said now, quietly, as snow fell on Bastogne and the young soldier who had never seen it before was all excited. "Jorgensen. My best pal in basic. He got such shit from the sergeant, fellow name of McCluskey. Government certified grade-A asshole. He'd decided Jorgensen was weak, was gonna wash out, and boy did he hound that poor sonofabitch." He sipped his whiskey and, thinking I'd better because I hadn't tried it since the first sip, I took a drink of mine. The melting ice had diluted it a little, and it stayed cold longer before the heat broke out deep in my chest. "So one night, after we'd drunk a little too much, we decided to play a little joke on McCluskey."

While I watched the men onscreen patrol in darkness that I knew had been shot in daylight, exchanging passwords and gunfire, my father told me how he and Jorgensen had managed to steal McCluskey's helmet and use it for a toilet bowl. They had figured he would discover the mess in the morning and have an unpleasant ten minutes cleaning it up. Satisfied with the prank, they had gone to bed expecting nothing more than an especially stormy inspection the next day. Someone, however, had planned a nighttime exercise, a drill involving sudden sirens and the order to assemble armed and prepared for combat, and, awakened and acting out of practiced habit, McCluskey had quickly shrugged into fatigues and checked his rifle's load. Last thing, on his way out to the assembly point, he had grabbed his shit-filled helmet and stuck it on his head. He arrived at his battle station with Jorgensen's and my father's gifts streaming down his face. My father laughed now and took another drink.

"I'll give him this, though, the sonofabitch," he said. "McCluskey kept that helmet on through that night's exercise."

"Did he know who did it? Did you guys get punished?"

"Way it works," he said, "is everyone's got everyone else's back. He couldn't say who'd shit in his helmet, we sure as hell weren't admitting it, and no one in the unit made a sound. Mc-Cluskey ran us ragged for a week, though. Jesus. I've never run so much in my life." He sipped again. "Why I can't imagine doing like you do. Running. I've never wanted to run another step in my goddamn life."

It was hard to follow the movie while listening to my father's story. The whiskey didn't help. I had not been sleepy before, and I was not exactly sleepy now, but after the second helping he poured into my glass, my eyelids were strangely heavy. One soldier ran away, it seemed, but then he turned up working in a kitchen somewhere behind the lines, in a village.

"What happened to them?" I said. "Jorgensen and the sergeant."

My father stared at the screen for a minute before he answered.

"Dead," he said. He poured more whiskey into his glass and drank before it had a chance to cool on the remaining ice. "Jorgensen, anyway. I never heard what happened to McCluskey, but he probably got fragged. Jorgy, though. Goddamndest thing. We were assigned to a quartermaster unit. Warehouse work. Behind the lines and safe as houses. I was in civvies by the time they shipped out, but Jorgensen was working in supply ops in country, on a base about as far from action as you could be. I thought, anyway. But the fucking gooks attacked it and Jorgy bought it. Might've been the mortar, might've been the ammo cooking off when it got shelled."

The soldier who had run away and then become a cook lay on the screen now, his eyes open and unmoving, his body pinned by the wall of the house by which the field kitchen had been set up. Neither of us said anything for a while, and when I'd finished drinking the whiskey in my glass, which got easier every sip, maybe, I thought, because whatever in my throat and chest had felt the burning from it had been burned out, my father poured another, even larger, glug into it. After some more fighting, the unit was relieved. They looked like hell, having lost some soldiers and endured days and nights of cold and enemy fire. But as they were limping back to safety behind the lines, seeing fresh troops heading into combat, the gruff sergeant straightened them up. He adjusted the butt of a cigar in his mouth and called the cadence, and the soldiers remaining in the unit stood up tall and marched in step and sang out in reply.

"Dad," I said. I could not remember when I had felt so comfortable with him or so close, and Andy's story prompted me to ask. "When your unit, the quartermaster unit, when it shipped out, why were you already in civvies? Why'd you leave the Army?"

He took a long time to answer. The credits ran on the television and a local ad for a used car dealer blared as he looked into his glass, at the wreckage of his toes in their gold-tipped socks.

"You," said. "I left the service because of you."

14.

FREE TIME, HE WALKS THE CAMPUS, pokes around the scruffy parts away from the mowed lawns and careful frontages. No place is allowed to get too overgrown, but weeds thrive in corners of the boundary wall and off the paths around the willow pond and down by the bus stop. He is wandering toward the bus stop now, putting off, he knows, some work he should be doing, whether in the naptime quiet of his room or the low hum of the library, when the squirrel bounds out from the high grass and freezes in front of him. They do this, squirrels, he has seen it often, jump or sprint into the path of something, then stop, sometimes to turn back, sometimes to run on again, some wired-in waywardness to trick a predator, perhaps, or some stupidity of the lower brain. Gabriel, though, just stops and stares, a daring stance, its little black eyes on his eyes, and what is even stranger is the way, as he watches the squirrel watching him, things flicker at the edges of his vision. The bus stop itself, an archaic edifice of brick sheltering the long green-painted bench, remnant of the long-ago age of students catching the bus into town and, from town, the train on to the city or the cities that were home, before everyone arrived on campus in a car, before the razing of the old infirmary to pave a parking lot. Faculty, too, would have taken the bus, up from the broad-lawned neighborhoods on the periphery of town, back, late in the afternoons, after the lectures and tutorials and conferences and meetings and, maybe, an hour of reading in the library, though now he sees Seymour and the others arriving, each alone, by car in the morning and departing, each alone, by car in the evening. The bus stop judders like film slipped from its sprockets, and in the barely visible half-seconds of slipping it ages suddenly, paint peeling and brick crumbling, weeds growing up around the pole on which the schedule should be posted but is not. They stand, gunslingers tautly watching for the tell-tale motion of a hand, until the squirrel, satisfied, breaks its gaze and, nodding—in acknowledgment? dismissal? sympathy?—runs off again.

Thing is, even though the squirrel is off pursuing its squirrelly life for the rest of the afternoon, the flickering continues. At the edges of his sight as he heads back to get some work done, to get a cup of tea, to get into the comfortable routine, some standard-issue nineteenth-century academic brick facades shudder into steel and glass, some storied buildings shrink to single, low-slung pre-fab. It takes an effort to keep things in focus, to keep his focus on things as they really are, the solid and familiar grounds, the quad and dorm and library. The slipping even follows him to his room, the standard wood bookcase with its neat rows of literary paperbacks jolting and jerking and, in momentary glimpses, suddenly a stack of catalogues and telephone directories. He has to squint, to concentrate so hard on keeping his surroundings still, that, finally, he stretches out atop the sheets, still in shoes and tweed jacket, and closes his eyes for an hour, after which things seem to have settled back into place.

15.

THE THING ABOUT THE 400 is that you run out of all the easy running two-thirds of the way around, so that for the last stretch you're running on fuel that isn't there. The first half feels pretty good, and if you could end the sprint directly across the field from where you'd started you would have some spring left in your legs, a little air still in your chest. Another hundred yards and everything is gone. "This," Coach said, "is when you have to run from deep. Draw your diaphragm down to pull air in. Soften your knees and tap strength from the core of your thighs, down by the bone. If you do it right, you end the lap not with a collapse but with a kick and you break the tape at your fastest pace." You might puke then, but there was time to stagger off to the side and retch your guts up after that fast finish. I used to note the weight and stiffness that set in at 300 meters and imagine my chest a bellows, my thighs burning hotter as the deep breaths fed the flames, consuming me so that I'd cross the line a column of ash, ready to fall into dust at the side of the track. That afternoon, the day before Thanksgiving, I hit the finish hard and tapped the stopwatch with my thumb, gasping and leaning on the chain-link fence, reading sixty-six seconds as bile rose behind my teeth. The stopwatch dangled from my hand as I stretched my calves and tried to slow my pulse. I could maybe save a second with a stronger start, staying lower for longer out of the blocks, and maybe I could shave part of another second with a harder kick. But the only way to get under a minute was to run faster all the way around the track.

Which was faster, to run like you were chasing something or to run like something was chasing you?

Thanksgiving had finally come, school ending early on this Wednesday and no teacher asking much beyond attendance and a minimum of violence, the Pirates out of the playoffs after last week's loss to Richland and the Toms restive with just the traditional Turkey Day Classic to go. In English, Mrs. Jansen had required a short essay, some to be read aloud in class, not on what students were thankful for because that was so fifth grade (though Reverend Alan's Young Life kids wore buttons that said "Thankful for Him," with a cross in the place of the "T") but, instead, on what we were thankful that we could stop doing. She, for one, was glad to see the end of Hester Prynne. "A for angel," she had muttered. "A for my ass." I had written that I was thankful not to have to see the red Ferrari lurking in the parking lot. I had watched my teacher walking unmolested every afternoon for the last couple of weeks to her sedate Celica and driving off in the direction of her library neighborhood. I had twice seen her out for dinner at the Pizza Hut with the heroic Bo. I had written, too, that I was thankful I could quit eating TV dinners with my father because my mother had come back from her Oklahoma sojourn and was overcooking round steak just as she had always done. I had quit sneaking up to Nicole Rose's window because she had made me promise to, had quit standing under the mimosa hoping for a glimpse of her, but I could not write that this made me thankful. I worried that I'd dreamed the silvery night with Nicole, I'd hardly seen her since, and not a syllable had passed between us, Heidi always right there at Nicole's side, whether she was driving the yellow Sunbird or standing and smoking with Nicole at the edge of the woods after school.

Sometimes on the TV coverage of the hostages, as the arm swung out to help the stumbling, blindfolded one, the voiceover would say something about status quo ante, how things were before the Shah was thrown out and the revolution took over the streets, the government, the lives of the people. Thanksgiving week felt like a return to the status quo ante, before the sight of Nicole stroking her breasts under the streetlight, before the nighttime ride with her on the handlebars, before I'd rescued Mrs. Jansen at the motel out on the old state highway. There was the new bonfire being planned, the Advent one, Mrs. Kramer and Reverend Alan hoping to prepare the way for the Savior by gathering up the Enemy's traces again and this time actually setting them ablaze. Status quo ante. It was like the track, always the same, the route never changing. But if you'd been around it once already, then it wasn't really the same, was it? Because the burning in your thighs and lungs and the sick feeling in your gut made this lap different from the last. Harder.

Or maybe this was just because, instead of heading home after the half-day to enjoy, like most kids, the free afternoon with friends, or to get away, like many, for a long weekend visiting family somewhere else, I was here at the track putting in laps, each harder than the last, the smoke from someone's happy holiday fire tickling my throat and chest so that, as I walked the straightaway to catch my breath, I hawked and, turning my head to spit, saw Mrs. Jansen walking toward the parking lot. So that I could watch her walk, I stretched my calves some more instead of kneeling to the blocks, and I saw her unlock the Celica and set her bag in the back seat. But instead of getting in and driving off, she glanced toward the street and over her shoulder at the school and then she shut the door and locked it again. I jogged in place. Faster when you were chasing something, because you knew that you could only catch it that way? Or when you were the one chased because desperation moved you as anticipation never could? Nothing to worry about because there was no sign of the Ferrari. It had taken a few days for the thumb-shaped bruise on my bicep to fade. No car came into the parking lot and Mrs. Jansen turned toward the track. I dropped to the start position, watching through the chain-link as she crossed the lot, not toward the track but toward one of the gaps between trees at the edge of the athletic fields. I rocked back on my heels and with my eyes followed her into the woods.

 None of my business. More than that. I was supposed to leave her business alone. I had been threatened, you had to admit, you had to call it that, though I supposed there was some way the doctor could claim otherwise. Hadn't I? And I needed to practice. And my gym bag, with my sweatshirt, was way back over by the bleachers.

 So of course I hopped the fence and entered the woods on a path I knew would meet the one Mrs. Jansen had taken, the trees easy to see through now that their leaves had fallen, a simple skein of limbs even where the brush between them made passing impossible. Mrs. Jansen walked fast, but she was not too far ahead, and, keeping her in sight, I figured I had to be heard, my every footfall finding fallen leaves to crunch, rifle-shot branches to snap, had to be heard but she never looked back and, instead, in the chilly breeze, held her jacket closed with both hands so that from behind it looked like she was praying as she walked. What are you praying for, Mrs. Jansen, help or forgiveness? I shivered, wishing I had taken the minute to jog back to the bleachers for my sweatshirt.

She stood at the edge of the ravine. On the other side, the clinic, the Ferrari, the doctor in his white lab coat, correcting the motion of a joint, making the children straight, and she would step down to the muddy relic of the Trinity's tributary and cross on the big stones and scramble up the other side, through the litter to the clinic lot and its dumpster and border of grime and cigarette butts and into the doctor's lab-coated arms, into the red car, out to the edge of town and the smoky motel room, and what business was it of mine, grownups were going to do what they were going to do, and I had ridden, run, to the rescue once, only to be thrown from the horse. Even I could tell that the motel was cheap. No bright drapery could make a Venice of the view over its parking lot and the highway and the warehouses along it, and how sexy could it be to stare up at the water stain on the ceiling, it made sense only as a place to stop, exhausted, on your way to someplace better, on the way to the border, maybe, part of an escape from all of this, but she did not want to escape so let her have the dingy room, pinned beneath the doctor, staring up at the water stain. It would be better if she were running away, at least, if she were carrying the bag that she would take with her, with the doctor, in his car, to the border, but instead she was just stepping up to the lip of the ravine in ridiculous shoes.

Mrs. Jansen went carefully, stopping each step to figure out the next, and for a while I could see her as she made her slow way down the slope. Once she had disappeared, I would go. I would turn away, turn back, return, run as I had planned, around the oval, and fuck them, her and Stark. She disappeared. I turned, and had taken the first step back toward the track when I heard a little scream and the sliding of a body down the side of the ravine, the scramble of a body struggling not to fall. I jogged to the end of the trail and looked over the edge to see her lying on her side halfway down, to watch her sit and rub her ankle, the broken shoe a little further down the slope. Well, at least she was on her way to an orthopedist. Mrs. Jansen looked across the ravine, looked down at her broken shoe, and, finally, looked back up the way that she had come, and said "William?"

Why was it people said your name as a question even when they knew perfectly well who you were. "William?"

"Are you okay?" I said. "Is your leg all right?"

She thought so, twisted ankle, stupid shoes, this was a dumb idea, this whole short cut through the woods, not her idea. She stopped. I was supposed to be descending now, I knew, holding out a hand to help her up, but I stayed where I was. Grownups were going to do what they were going to do and I had ridden once to the rescue only to be unhorsed. Yes, she went on, a really dumb idea and there was going to be a big stain on her skirt, she'd have to Shout it out, like in the commercials, and still I did not move. Did I not see that she could use a hand? Did she really have to ask?

"When he," I said, nodding across the ravine, "your friend, gave me a ride, he told me stay away. He was really clear about it." I had been told to mind my business, and my business now was at the track, shaving seconds off my laps. I needed to get back, grateful for that tip the doctor had given me, everything moving along the same straight line, no wasted motion. She looked smaller down there, fragile. I shivered.

"William?"

"I have to run," turning though my joints screamed, lifting my feet and setting them on the path back toward the track, toward the oval, toward my business. She had gotten herself into this, had fallen down the slippery slope like someone out of Reverend Alan's sermons, and she'd just have to get herself back out. There were roots and rocks to grasp, and if she had to hobble her way back to the silver Celica, well at least she knew a good man for bones and joints. That the wind was suddenly colder and seemed to slice into my chest just meant that there was a front coming through and that eventually, even here in Centertown, fall had to turn to winter. That the bare limbs creaked and scraped and clacked meant only that the breeze was getting stronger, anything else was pathetic. I had to get back to the track.

Would I have made it out of the woods and gone to run my race if I had not heard her crying, if, after the little grunt as she stood and the muttered curse and "ow" as she settled her weight on the twisted ankle, there had been only the noise of her ascent, the sound of someone managing her way back up the slope? When those sounds stopped, when all I heard, still only steps from the edge, just out of the teacher's sight, when all I heard was the heavy exhalation that might, if I did not know better, be just another sibilance of chilly wind kicking the dead leaves, I stopped, and when the heavy breath grew husky and harsh, when a plaintive keening pressed through the rush of air, I turned and walked back to see her sitting with her elbows on her knees, her face in her hands.

I stepped my own way down the slope.

"Can you stand up?"

She could, with my help, and when she was on her feet we stood, for so long my calves began to cramp, and she wept against my chest, smearing my T-shirt and shuddering in my arms until the storm inside her blew itself out and the tremors were no more than the flutter of some internal butterflies' wings. Mrs. Jansen took a deep breath and settled back into herself, stepping away from me, careful to keep her footing on the slope.

"I got your shirt snotty."

"I can help you," I said. "Where do you want to go?"

That was the question, wasn't it? I must know where she had been going, both of us looking, as she spoke, across toward the clinic parking lot, but this fall, you didn't have to be a poetry teacher to see a sign there, did you, not that she believed in signs, but boy when the outward and visible is a tumble into the slough, when it breaks your shoe and cripples you, this as we stood, my arm supporting her, on the slope, when it leaves you abandoned between two places, two people, two possible ways that you could be, you might want to pay attention. So, yes, where to go? Back in the safety of the school or even of the Celica, she could get off her feet, figure out how bad her ankle was, clean the mud from her leg and skirt. But she could do all that on the other side, too, where Paul was waiting, and he might come looking if she didn't show up, was getting insistent, impatient with her. I shivered.

"God," she said. "You must be freezing."

"We should go," she said. I needed to get inside, get home, someone must be waiting for me, too, but I was okay and if she didn't know yet where she wanted to go, I had an idea. I took her weight on my shoulders, stepping carefully up and bringing her with me to the top of the ravine, pulling her after me once I was up, and not far, then, to the tight grove of brush-clad oaks. I half-led and half-carried her there and, inside, settled her on the fallen trunk.

"It's kind of magical," she said. "From outside, you'd never think you could get in here. You wouldn't think there's an *in here* to get to."

I gathered some of the sticks that littered the ground and arranged them in a teepee. There was no paper or anything to start the fire, there were none of the brown bags in which Fats had smuggled snack cakes, none of the newspaper pages in which he had sometimes wrapped thick sandwiches. I opened the foot locker on the coverless nudie mag and the big poetry book Mrs. Jansen had lent me. She smiled, saying that someone had finally found a use for naked photographs. The magazine pages did not catch well from the flame of her lighter.

"Tear out some of the poetry," she said. "It might make something happen after all."

I flipped through, randomly, until she said "There. Tear that out. Keats."

"You don't like Keats?"

"I adore Keats," she said. "Especially the odes. But I know his poems by heart, so we don't need them in the book." She closed her eyes. "'I see a lily on thy brow, with anguish moist and fever-dew, and on thy cheeks a fading rose fast withereth too.'

Oh, you'll love Keats someday, I know it. And Rilke. You should learn German just so you can read Rilke. He's untranslatable sometimes. '*Jeder Engel is schrecklich.*'"

Fed with the onionskin pages, the fire got going and I said we would not set the thicket aflame, I knew. Fats and I had sat around many fires here without roasting ourselves. She picked up leaves from around her feet, poking the stem of one through the lobe of another, linking them.

"Sorry," she said. "For falling apart." I had fallen down that slope myself, I told her, had fallen here and elsewhere plenty of times, and nothing hurt like a twisted ankle. It wasn't her ankle, she said, closing the circle in the garland she was making and setting it on her head. Oh the things you could make out of leaves.

"In elementary school," I said, "we did this craft around this time of year, for Thanksgiving. You picked up leaves at recess and they gave you wax paper and you'd arrange the leaves between two sheets." She nodded, yes, of course, she knew this craft, the teacher helping each student to lay the leaf sandwich on a makeshift ironing board, to lay a cloth over the wax paper and lightly run a hot iron over to make the wax sheets stick together.

"Placemats."

"We've got all the ones I ever made. My mom could set the table for tomorrow with them."

She shivered and I was warmer now, by the fire. Did she want to come closer? But no, she said, she wasn't cold, that wasn't it.

"He picked me up once, in the parking lot," she nodded toward it. "It was late enough there wasn't really anyone around, but you can't be too careful, right? So I was slumped way down and lying with my head on his leg. I could feel the muscle in his thigh move, every little movement it made, as he pressed the gas or let up on it, and I was kind of in the way when he was shifting, so I could see the cuff of his shirt and the way it circled his wrist and the way the tendons moved as he shifted gears. My face was resting on his thigh and I could feel the fabric of his pants and god it was the nicest material and I thought, and this was still early on, maybe the third or fourth time we slept together, we hadn't been sneaking around for very long, I thought it was so strange that the loveliest feeling I had as I was lying there with my head in my lover's lap was the sensation of that fabric against my skin. He buys the absolute nicest pants."

If I could point to some spell she'd cast to enthrall me, I might resist, but here she sat, mud on her skirt and her hair a mess, crowned with the leaf garland, her mascara settled in dark half-rings beneath her eyes, staring into the meager fire as if she were under some spell herself, and maybe she was, caught by some magic woven through the doctor's pants, and so I knelt in front of her and the teacher opened her jacket and took me to her. My head resting on her breast, feeling its soft fall and swell, awakened to the deep unrest of her scent, the dried-herb smell of her perfume, and she held me, her arms and hands spreading warmth over my back, and what was the name for this feeling, my penis hard and my lips burning even as my throat closed and the tears burned as they gathered in the corners of my eyes?

"I don't know what to do with all my tenderness," I said, as she stroked my hair and pulled me closer, whispering, yes, yes, it was so hard, it was just so fucking hard. There was the silver Celica, not far away, the sweatshirt at the track, a change of clothes in the bag I'd left by the bleachers and by the time anyone came looking for us we'd be halfway to Mexico. "Oh sweetie," she said and she kissed the top of my head and squeezed my ear between her finger and thumb, the most intimate touch I had ever felt. "Oh sweetie," she said. "If only, if only." There was no getting away, there was only this moment in the elfin grot, this place away from the pale kings and riders, and how, as she whispered, I came to be kissing her or her to be kissing me, I could not tell which, I could not tell, her hand holding me, pressing or allowing me to press, I could not tell, but she was whispering, "Just this, just now, yes, yes." It was okay, she said, and I cried out against her lips and she took my cry into her mouth with her tongue and gave it back to me in a whisper, kissing, again saying that yes, it was okay.

"I love you," I said, after, resting my head on her breast, her fingers idle in my hair.

"Oh no you don't," she said.

16.

WILLOUGHBY KNOWS ALL THE CURRENT THINKING ON TIME TRAVEL, *unknown dimensions inclined to irrupt into our everyday reality, multiple universes laminated one over another and another over that, with, always, the slight chance of some snag in the fabric, some leaking of one into another. He is not inclined to talk about these ideas, though, intent, instead, on a new strategy he is unfolding move by move the next afternoon. The only space-time fold at stake is the one he is creating with the wholesale sacrifice of high-value pieces, the cavity opening up along the right side of the king's court. A trap, clearly, though it is hard to see what Willoughby will have left to spring on him if he slides into it. He keeps his finger on a bishop, asking, again, whether that could be it, some quantum irresolution setting up this shimmer of alternatives, then thinks better of the move and puts the bishop back. Willoughby glares. Is this a chess game or a physics seminar? Look, there is a whole philosophical literature on time and they could talk about that, sure, but if so then they ought to put the pieces up and stop pretending that they're playing. Okay, okay, a playing-for-time knight move far from the action mollifying Willoughby for the moment, though, still irritated, Willoughby grunts and throws his queen out into a whole intersecting set of fatal vulnerabilities. It could, though, couldn't it, be something like that, some world in which their beloved campus is some wholly other kind of place, in which the two of them, this very moment, might be doing something not at all like playing chess, might, even, never have met at all?*

Conceding the possibility, Willoughby also concedes the game, flicking his king over with an over-long and slightly grimy nail. This timing is not bad. A couple of undergraduates have decided to serenade the room with a duet by the bookcase, to the consternation of the room's more studious occupants. "Rose, rose," they sing. "When will I see thee, when?" Tension and volume are rising together, the rumble of irritation an awkward counterpoint to the singers' complicated descant. Willoughby retreats into the speculations central to his thesis and as the prefects move to restore order, an hour or so back in the room organizing the surface of the desk and working at his essay seems like the right course. These singers themselves are starting to sound shrill, all the jackets and sweaters starting to take on the pilled dishevelment of bathrobes and pajamas.

    Problem is, someone, it seems, has been in his room. The pad he left neatly ninety-degreed in the center of his desk has been shifted, and where he had stopped his careful pencil script mid-line a red crayon scrawl rips the middle of the page from nape to navel, spilling its guts in warning: "what can ail thee so haggard and so woebegone?" Like the glued stack of sheets, the red scrawl layers this line over roses on snow, one red bleeding through another white, and the sense of violation—someone has been at his desk!—sets the oscillation going, this world and that other, grimmer, dingier, fallen one spinningly switching before his blinking eyes. He falls away from his desk as if the scrawl-split pad has struck him. It's a threat, he can see that even as he shuts his eyes against the stack of slack, fat paperbacks, the sweater hanging from a plastic hook, the shaped plastic chair that clatters as he shoves himself away, a threat someone has left here, in his room, on his desk, but who has any cause to threaten him? "What can ail thee" grows up, beanstalk or magic rose bush, a thicket of woven bramble in which he cowers, haggard and woebegone, cradling roses gathered on a bed of snow.

    Who, though, Dr. Seymour asks, tapping ash and leaning back in her chair, would break in and leave such a note? He is not sure "leave a *note" captures this violation. He has felt gutted and dizzy for the couple of days since he found the crayoned phrases. Why that language, Dr. Seymour wonders. Does he recognize it? Something he's read, he thinks, something he dimly remembers, a knight, a lady, everybody very pale. It's a spell, she says. Does he know anything about magic? Does he know how spells are cast? Such things were included neither in his high school curriculum nor in his courses here at college, nothing, at least, beyond some memorized chanting of a toxic recipe, some bubbling and troubling over a cauldron. Magic, she says, is misunderstood. It is thought of as the calling forth of demons or the imposition of one's will on the fabric of the world, but it's really more a matter of focus. Harmony. In the practice of magic, properly understood, one simply paid attention to the forces at work in things, and then brought energy and concentration to bear on a pressure point, like a geological fault, not to violate those forces but to alter them slightly, to shift their course toward one's own desired ends. It's like sailing. Has he ever sailed? He has not. She's no sailor herself, a jet of smoke up toward the ceiling corner, where it unravels, a spiral widening, dissipating, disappearing in the shadow that seems always to be gathering there, but the principle is simple enough. Say you want to cross from point A to point B but the wind is coming from B toward A. You can get to your destination, but not by just setting out into the face of the wind. Instead, you tack, turning the sail to take advantage of, oh, complicated things. Slipstreams, physics. It takes a while, maybe, but with care and patience the boat can be sailed across and against the wind. A spell is a sort of spiritual tacking. One pays attention, finds the forces, their vectors, intuits the fault line, slipstream, and, often with some atmospheric help—she waves her cigarette, tobacco is one among the dried leaves often burnt to create that atmosphere, not that she is one for casting spells—and with some object as the outward and visible focal point for the concentration, one, hmm, nudges.*

"I'm being nudged?"

"It's interesting to me that you described the crayon writing as a rip. That suggests a fabric to be torn through, a veil, maybe, to be rent." She stands and goes to the window, where curtains are parted and tied back, a translucent scrim down to keep out the brightest of the sunlight, to keep the room invisible to anyone who might be peering in from outside. The knight, she says, is enchanted. Enthralled. He doesn't realize it at first because he can only see, in his mind or his memory, the lady who has brought him away, the lady with whom he has dallied. Dr. Seymour raises the shade, the hues outside now brighter, the outlines of leaves, trunks, students crossing the lawn, more sharply defined. He's under her spell, but the pale kings and princes have their own intention, and when that intention breaks through the lady's enchantment, the knight sees himself anew, sees himself more clearly and as he really is.

"You remind me of her," he says, and when she asks if he means la bell dame he says no, the woman in his essay, the one he has dreamed of, the one who brings roses in the snow. Was she English? No, not that. Nothing so immediate. It's more, he gazes up into the dissipating smoke, atmospheric.

"Your revision," she says. "That's got you thinking about words, yes? Layers of meaning?" Of course. She pulls the scrim back down over the window. "Veil is the root of revelation. To reveal, to make visible what has been hidden by removing what veils the truth. All right? All right. We think of our language as a means of revelation. We speak, we write, whatever. We communicate, bringing the truth from one mind to another. But language is like a wind. Its dominant direction is troubled by eddies, back-currents. These may seem like impurities, distractions to be ignored or ironed out, but they are opportunities. Our stories are spells, woven of words, cast over the world. They are the windows, often curtained, often *veiled, through which we see. But they bear within themselves these flaws or faults, and, if we focus on these, we might cast a new spell, shift the forces slightly to reveal. With me?"*

What ails him? There is no enchantment here, no magic, though he has, since he arrived, found delightful every aspect of the campus, of his interactions with faculty and fellow students. No spell has been cast, none needs to be cast. What, he does not ask aloud, is she talking about? At the heart of the story is the rose blooming red upon the snow, an emblem, love and warmth and joy even in barren winter. Someone has vandalized his page, violated his privacy. What the hell is she talking about?

"Okay. This talk of spells is taking us away from the point." She sits on her side of the desk again. "Let's get back to the task at hand. Revision. What does that mean? To revise?"

"Well, easy," he says. "It means to improve something. You assigned the essay, I wrote the essay, you say to revise it and I try to make it better."

"Not bad," she says. "Not quite right, but not bad." She writes the word, revision, on the pad on her desk, draws a slash through it, and turns the pad toward him. Re/vision. "The vision here is the same as the vision you see with, and the re is the same as the re in repeat. Re/vision: to see again. When I was a student, back in Britain, we spent periods of each school year on revision, by which we meant what students here call studying. To revise there was to look over, to take a new view of the material you had spent the year working through. The idea is the same. When we revise, we see again, see anew. And this is what we're working on in your writing. I'm asking you to see again, to see in a new way, the image you've built your work around. And I think something in you is working its way into the slipstream, some intention you're not aware of is trying to shift the forces from their current direction. And this is not unusual. Writers talk about it all the time."

It dawns on him that she thinks he *crayoned that slash across the page. It dawns on him that maybe she did it, strange as it is to imagine a distinguished campus figure sneaking, breaking, into a student's room in order to cast, to break, a spell.* "What is it," she says.

"What ails me, do you mean?"

17.

NO, I DIDN'T, SHE HAD SAID, BUT DIDN'T I? What was love if not the mingling of, on the one hand, this electricity along the skin, this strange static dancing in the nerves and sending, at moments of contact, moments, even, of sufficient nearness, sparks of such brightness that all the dark byways and corridors were lit up and the ways through illuminated, imprinting on the blinking eyes after, and, on the other, the cleaving of the chest and the revelation of what lay there, not the stubborn heart that people talked about, a muscle clenching to drive the mere meat of being, but the kernel of eternal wound, the open and bleeding need that recognized itself in the unstoppable and corresponding need of the other? Here, I had known from early on, was no place that did not see me and like the subjects of surveillance I had seen in science fiction films and read of in Orwell, I had been seen at every second by the prying eyes of parents, peers, and all who got their little bit of power through what they knew of me, through the humiliating glimpse that could be rewound through the sprockets and projected on the walls of school or any social space. You stumbled and were scolded, limped and were laughed at, known and at the mercy of the ever open and all seeing eyes of Centertown. You thought what you wanted was not to be seen. You became acquainted with the night in order to avoid the watchman's gaze, when, all along, what had been leaking endlessly into the innermost cavities of body and soul was a need precisely to be seen but to be seen and shown at the same moment the opened chest and, in it, the shocking shred of need that was just like your own.

That there might be the taste of lips and tongue, the shocking touch, the brilliant inextinguishable satisfaction at, in, on the gentle hand, was, I would be the first to say, a welcome adjunct to the primary connection.

All of this was clear to me throughout the evening, clear as I helped with pies and preparation for the next day's dinner, as I felt with the seismograph's sensitivity the pressure of familial faults as the television mindlessly reminded no one watching that the hostages would not be spending this Thanksgiving with their families and then consoled no one watching with three hours of rerun cops chasing rerun criminals. Clear, too, was the reason for Nicole's retreat, because there was a frightening element in this matter of being seen and known and no doubt she could use some reassurance. And so it was I found myself, for the first time, standing not under the mimosa in the Rose front yard and not in the cramped space between the air-conditioning compressor and Nicole's window, but, instead, at the front door, the one from which I had seen, without quite seeing, Nicole emerge on that September night, found myself knocking and rehearsing my speech, fingering the envelope into which I had stuffed the allusive and articulate outpouring of my tenderness.

A woman, clearly too old to be Nicole's mother, maybe her grandmother, answered and looked on uncomprehendingly as I stammered "Nicole?" and then, leaving the door ajar, turned away and disappeared, calling to someone in the holiday smells of baking inside. It had seemed wrong to write my declaration on notebook paper or, the other option, PC Office Supply Co.

stationery. The postcard—the famous façade of the Alamo shot against a purple evening sky, souvenir of the seventh-grade trip to San Antonio, the one on which Fats had thrown up at the back of the bus and we had ridden back to the Metroplex in a vomitous miasma—was the best I could find and it fit awkwardly into the envelope. I had tried to smooth my hand, a scrawl of Bic ballpoint for which I was constantly scolded in the margins of my homework, even, especially, by Mrs. Jansen, but it was, I hoped, the thought rather than the loops and lines of awkward cursive that mattered. She would be able to read the words, to read the depth of feeling beneath them. At the approach of footsteps, I felt all the words I had prepared to speak depart my mind, and I was holding the envelope in front of me as stiffly as a butler carrying cards in on a salver when Hector threw the door wide open and stared at me, saying "'Sup?"

There was, in every line of Hector's face and body, evidence of ease. What could it be like to move through the world, as Hector did, unworried about how the world was looking at you? Had he ever felt the yearning that had built in me so that the momentary pressure of Mrs. Jansen's hand had loosed torrents of understanding? It was obvious, just looking at Hector as he stood, framed by the doorway and slightly backlit, that any time he felt a little itch, a little build-up, say, that was starting to make his pants feel tight, he knew the world was built so that he could take care of it. "No Muff Too Tuff," as his tight T-shirt proclaimed. Worst case, as I had seen, as I could never forget seeing, Hector would use his sister, but the smooth movement of muscle under the shirt and the way he leaned against the doorjamb told the most casual observer that things rarely got to that point. The familiarity with bodies and backseats told itself in Hector's every gesture and if the world was watching then Hector must see himself the star of his own highlight reel.

In the face of the muscles, the mustache, and the impassive information that Nicole was not at home, I undertook to retreat, mumbling that I could try another time, sorry to bother, was just in the neighborhood, but "No, dude," Hector said, and was that envelope for her because he could take it and even as I shook my head, the envelope was plucked from my reluctant grasp. The promise—threat?—of prompt delivery hung still in the air with the shortening grease and the aroma of sweating onions and baking pumpkin and, had I heard that right, the whispered "Pussy" as the door swung closed and I would never get to apologize for the sloppiness of the seal, the illegibility of my missive. I had not yet gotten out of the yard when the yellow Sunbird rounded the corner and coasted to the curb, the girl emerging almost before it had stopped not the one with whom I had ridden the midnight streets of Centertown only a week or so before. Armored in a black leather jacket and jeans, helmed in a shellac of back-pulled, cinched black hair, and masked in makeup, this was the Nicole I had known before I came to know Nicole. She looked older than Mrs. Jansen, untouchable, unapproachable, her cheekbones marked with rouge, her lips outlined and glossed, her eyelids weighted down with shadow, a whole catalogue of impossibilities. Only when her eyes moved quickly between me and the closing front door did the mask slip, maybe, a little, before the visor fell back into place and she stabbed me with an icy, "What are you doing here?"

She didn't wait for an answer, but stalked past me as I hung up on a first syllable whose second I could not find in the atmosphere suddenly airless with perfume and smoke, exhaust and contempt.

"I-I-I," Heidi sang as she passed in Nicole's wake. "Ab-ab-ab. Ga-ga."

The Thanksgiving Day game was meaningless, the season over and the Pirates out of the playoffs. It contributed nothing to the standings. Centertown came out to kill the time the turkey took to roast and families who had watched their sons and brothers ride the bench all season at last got to see them play. On banners as on the bumper stickers that had shown up on cars around town, Mickey Mouse shouted at Iran and raised his middle finger. The snack bar offered Frito pies even at ten in the morning and, ignoring the game and enjoying a minute away from my father and Uncle Earl, I had just taken a bite of mine when a hand tapped my shoulder. I turned, swallowing, to see neither Mrs. Jansen, for whom I had looked out all morning, turning to scan the bleachers between plays, nor Nicole Rose, whom I had never seen at a game and so had not expected to see here. Instead, Kramer's mother widened her smile and said hello, it had been such a long time. She had been room mother when her son Craig and I were in the third grade. My, how time flew now, all those boys and girls grown up and high school students and how was I doing on this blessed day? I said I was fine and happy Thanksgiving to her too and yes I was sure this snack would not spoil my dinner.

"Listen, William, I have to ask you something a teensy bit nosey, but as a member of the P.T.A. it's the kind of thing I really can't not ask about, okay?"

Her hair was drawn back in a motherly pony tail and tied with a school-colors ribbon that matched her school-colors jacket. She had been at Payne yesterday, she told me, oh for another meeting, there were nothing but meetings these days, about dress codes and reading lists and things of that nature, and she could have sworn that she saw, as she came out of the building in the afternoon, me emerging from that little scrap of wasteland beyond the track and the parking lot. And was that Mrs. Jansen I had been walking with, helping to walk, even? Had she hurt herself, poor thing? And whatever had the two of us been doing back there? Didn't I know that a group of Satanists did their evil rituals down there in those sewer ditches, murdering cats and getting up to the Devil's work?

"Cross country," I said, hiding my lying lips behind a napkin as I pretended to wipe chili from my mouth.

Then she was going to have to have a word with the coach because surely it was unsafe to have students running through that tangle of grapevine and garbage, but no, I said, it had not been an official practice, not on the day before Thanksgiving. I was just running back there on my own. Training. *It really couldn't be a good idea,* Mrs. Kramer smiled her leaden smile, not that she had ever been back in those woods, not since she was a girl anyway, when they had extended much farther, but there must be roots and rocks, and from what she had heard from her Craig, the woods were filled with broken glass and things. Perhaps she should urge my parents to caution me against running in those woods. They were a hazard and she had been hoping for years that someone would bulldoze them. Just imagine if you built a cute little shopping plaza there, you could even put in a little malt shop where students could go for ice cream after school, and wasn't that my father over there in the bleachers?

Well, that wasn't going to make me nervous. My father knew I ran all kinds of places and he wasn't going to care that one of them was the acre of scrub behind the school. Mrs. Kramer seemed to get this without me saying a word and what she really couldn't understand, she went on, and maybe I had some insight on this, was what *Mrs. Jansen* had been doing out there. She wasn't on the cross country team, after all.

"It was a squirrel," I said before I had time to think of anything better. She had seen it, Mrs. Jansen, on the way to her car, a squirrel, hurt somehow and limping into the woods. It had maybe been hurt by some kids, kicked or hit by something somebody had thrown at it. I wasn't sure. She hadn't been clear about it. It was easy enough to imagine, though, I could see, even as I made it up, the Toms gathered around a trapped and panicked rodent, closing off every avenue of escape, kicking it back and forth like a furry soccer ball.

"A hurt squirrel?"

Oh, yes, I told her. Mrs. Jansen had been quite upset by it and hoped that if we found it we might get it to a vet or something.

"A vet?"

"Anyway," I said, "we scrambled through the woods after it. But even hurt, the squirrel moved too fast for us. We lost it in the underbrush."

"And then?"

And then, well, she hadn't really been wearing the right shoes for running around in the woods, Mrs. Jansen, and she had slipped and hurt her ankle. I had just helped her back to her car, and that must have been when Mrs. Kramer saw us, both disappointed, of course, that we had been unable to help the squirrel, which was doubtless dead by now, from its injuries or from the tender mercies of a cat or dog or whatever might go after a wounded squirrel in the woods.

"She is a very sensitive young woman, yes," Mrs. Kramer said. But, as the ankle injury showed, she might be well advised to focus her sympathies a little more and leave the suffering of squirrels to the Lord. "His eye is on the sparrow, after all," but it felt, as she stared at my face, like the eye she had in mind did not belong to the Lord.

There was always something needed from the store at the last minute on Thanksgiving, something that had been forgotten on the big shopping trip the weekend before or, often, something that I had eaten without realizing that it was for the holiday dinner. The discovery of this need was accompanied, every year, by raised voices, by the knock of a pan or dish against the counter, the slam of a door and the screech of tires. This time it was dinner rolls. They came in packages of twelve, on their own little trays that could go in the oven, and needed just a few minutes to heat through and brown on top. Everyone loved them and it wouldn't be Thanksgiving without them, but somehow they had not made into the cart as my mother had steered it through the crowded Kroger aisles. She distinctly and loudly remembered telling me to pick up a couple of packages of the rolls, but my mind always wandered, what was my problem these days, and I must have forgotten. I'd got the wrong brand of canned cranberry sauce, too. Somebody, then, was going to have to run up to the 7-11 and see if they had some. They wouldn't be the right brand, probably, but they would have to do. My father was not about to go, he was in the middle of adding the leaf to the table and getting in the extra chairs from the garage. The women couldn't leave the kitchen, not just as everything was coming to the crucial point, not if anybody in this house wanted to eat dinner before the Cowboys kicked off, and so "Come on, boy," Earl grumbled, "I'll drive. You get the goddamn rolls and I'll see if there's some way to restock the beer while we're at it."

There was no way to restock the beer while we were at it. The six-packs beckoned from behind clear cooler doors, but those doors were locked for the holiday, a time during which attention, at the invitation of the state, chastening and hastening its will to make known, should focus on gratitude for gifts and plenty. Earl swore and said he'd be in the car. I found two packages of dinner rolls, the last two, on the shelf, and, sure enough, they weren't the right ones but they were all the store had. I bought them and I was just stepping through the door when the yellow Sunbird squealed into the little lot. Heidi, in a too-big jacket and sunglasses, got out, the engine still running, and, never turning toward me, never turning her head anywhere, shouldered her way straight into the store.

Nicole was in the passenger seat. She wore sunglasses, too, her only mask now, last night's makeup gone and her hair hanging loose, some strands curtaining her cheek, and she seemed to have eyes only for whatever was straight through the windshield. Her window was partway down and before I had really chosen to do so I found myself walking to the yellow car, the packages of dinner rolls held to my chest, saying, as I got close, "I don't understand," and hearing Nicole say, quietly, "Just go, you just have to go," and, emerging from the store with a Pepsi and two packs of Marlboro Lights, Heidi saying, shrilly, "Oh my fucking God."

What, she went on, the fuck was the matter with me? Could I not take a hint? Could I not understand a direct fucking request? Nicole didn't want to talk to me. She didn't want to hear from me. She didn't want to see me stalking around her house in the middle of the night like a fucking pervert peeking fucking Tom, yeah, that's right, she knew about that. She set the bottle and the cigarettes on top of the car and opened the driver's side door. Whatever I thought had happened between me and Nicole, it hadn't happened and I should get that through my head. And this letter writing? Stop. *Shine boy for her acid brat?* What the fuck did that even mean? What was I fucking talking about? What was the fucking matter with me?

"Leave her alone," she said.

The few other people who had been inside the store or going in or out of it had gathered on the curb, though they hadn't really needed to. Heidi's voice echoed against the empty pavements of the holiday streets and closed shop-fronts and hung like smoke in the cold and cloudless sky. "Leave her alone and if I see you anywhere near Nicole I will personally drag your pants down and cut your dick off."

Then she was in the car and it shot into the empty street, the bright square of Alamo postcard, its reverse side covered with my careful cursive, floated in its exhaust and came to rest on the yellow line between the lanes. By the end of the afternoon, before the Cowboys had finished losing to the Oilers, the card would be pulped by the tires of those few cars that passed there, on their way to or from a happier family dinner than the one I would endure.

"Damn," Earl grinned as I slumped in the passenger seat. "What did you do to that girl, son? What did you do?"

18.

HIS BOOK IS SITTING ON THE BENCH BESIDE HIM. *He brought it along thinking he would spend an hour here reading as the afternoon dims toward evening and the last of the color drains and dies in the deepening gray. Instead, he has been watching. It comes in spells. Not the kind Dr. Seymour was talking about; he doesn't believe in that kind, or didn't, though now he has, perhaps, doubts. It comes in spells like fainting or dizziness. The oscillation, at first, was rapid, flickering, uncontrollable. He was blinded by the sudden juddering in which the campus and this other, unfamiliar institution switched places second after second. Now, though, if he relaxes and blurs the focus in his eyes, he can, not quite control but, instead, slow the shutter speed and in those spells during which the other place irrupts through the familiar campus he can start to study them. The low glass and concrete structures, the leaf-littered and ragged patches of grass shot across by crumbling concrete. Worst of all, there flicker into visibility, from time to time, in isolate seconds, ghostly shapes, his fellow students replaced by wandering, shrouded, blank-faced figures.*

When he refocuses—it's hard, he has to concentrate—and brings the present campus back, the squirrel, Gabriel, the big one, the bully, is standing across the paved path, standing upright, black claws poised over the top of the scar as if ready to pull it open, drawing the dingy fur back like drapes, and when it sees him notice, the squirrel seems, again, to nod at him. He wants to dive across the path right now and stamp the thing to death, but he'd never catch it in the open. Any sudden move now will destroy the little trust he's built up with stolen cookies. Instead, he picks up the book he brought along to read, something to study for the week's tutorials. He can't remember now which book he grabbed as he left his room, something that promised to absorb him for an idle hour. In his hands now, though, is a mid-1970s volume of the Waco, Texas, Yellow Pages. Someone is playing tricks on him, someone or something, student or squirrel or the simple fact of distraction.

"I've got it," he says over the chessboard a few days later. Willoughby looks incurious, his eyes on a bishop around which he has been developing a new attack. "It's not a different world, a parallel universe. I know you said the physics would support the notion, but it doesn't feel like that, like a space-time fold or whatever." The flickering is constant now but he can, for a little while at least, keep it at bay, keep it, at least, restricted to the corners of his eyes if he squints, physically and mentally, narrows his attention to what's right in front of him. In the periphery, the shrouds sway and moan. "Or maybe it is another world, just not another world in the sense meant by you scientists." He thwarts Willoughby, for the moment, with a knight's risky foray. He'll have to walk the knight back in a minute, once Willoughby's rook gets a clear line. You know how there are theories about residual presences? A kind of lingering energy after something happens, after someone leaves or dies? The place that crops up through campus, or settles over it, like dust covers over furniture, it's vague. It's got no texture. It's a place where things once happened but they're not happening anymore. Same thing with the figures. Willoughby is irritated, wants to concentrate on the attack, on opening up a line for that rook. These shrouds, they're emanations, smears of energy. They used to be connected to people, maybe, but they're left behind. They bring the featureless place with them. It's their place, the place they moved through. "No, I haven't figured out why or where or how. But Willoughby." He lowers his voice as some of the shrouds by the window—not the *wood-framed mullioned panes he knows are there but, in the corner of his eye, a plain sheet of thick glass staring out onto a few yards of dead grass and a handful of branched trees—moan louder.* "Willoughby, I think," *as his opponent insistently ignores him and, for a fraction of a second, flickers and is, though the glimpse is too brief to be believed, one of the shrouds himself,* "I think they're ghosts."

That night, the squirrel comes all the way in, used, now, to following crumbs from the brick ledge onto the neat desk, where he places the biggest, butteriest, choicest fragment. It holds his eyes with the glittering black of its own. He cannot tell which of them is tempting and entrancing which. He feels frozen, paralyzed, unable even to break the stare as the squirrel rests its claws in the cleft in its chest and begins to open the furred flesh there, to draw it back like curtains, to reveal. He shakes himself awake, the squirrel, mid-nibble, startles and skitters for the open window, is a final fluff of tail in the lamplight as it leaps for the branch beyond. The room slips into that gray and grainy ghost room until he brings to bear on it all of the force his mind can muster, an act of concentration that feels physical, a hard push against the inside of his forehead, and it swivels back to normal, his books neatly shelved, his jacket hung where it is supposed to hang, the desk its usual right angles, neat except for the last crumbs of cookie, which he sweeps now into his hand and drops into the trash.

19.

"GO ON," MRS. JANSEN SAID. "OPEN IT."

It was too early for presents. The hallways were hung with construction-paper evergreens and the math classroom boasted a poster reading "Hark, the Herald Angle's Sine!" but gifts were usually a last-day-before-vacation thing.

She had asked me to come by her room after school and when I had arrived she had said we had to leave the door open, didn't want to feed the rumor mills, and then handed me the little gift-wrapped box. I didn't have anything for her, I said, but that was okay, this wasn't really a Christmas present, more of a thank-you. I stripped off the paper and opened the white cardboard box. Lying on the tuft of cotton inside was a stone squirrel. I took it out and set it on Mrs. Jansen's desk. The squirrel stood on its hind legs, its front paws before its chest as if it were holding a nut or about to unzip its fur, a demented expression on its face, carved eyes staring and the mouth curved in an angry grin.

"Squirrel, eh?"

"I know." I shook my head. "It was all I could think of. She ambushed me."

Well, it was better than, she didn't say "the truth" but I knew that was how the sentence ended, and anyway none of it was Mrs. Kramer's business, not that that was ever going to get in that woman's way. She was still upset that her public burning had been snuffed out. Mrs. Jansen picked up the squirrel.

"It's kind of demonic, I know," she said. "It's Mexican." She thought maybe there weren't the same kind of squirrels there, in Cancún, where she had bought it years ago, when she and Bo were a happy couple. She set the squirrel back on the desk and said that had been a really happy trip.

"I've never been to Mexico," I said, and oh, she said, I had to go. I had to see the pyramids and Teotihuacan and the beautiful buildings in Cuernavaca and I'd be astonished, just as she had been, at the size of Mexico City, at the way it just went on and on in every direction. And of course there were the beaches. But she hadn't been back herself, not since that trip to Cancún.

"Why not?"

"Because there are always fires to put out, William."

She laid the squirrel back in its cotton bed and fitted the lid onto the box. I zipped the gift up in my backpack.

"Last week," she said.

"I know," I said, the magical half-hour already fading to sepia and settling into a frame, a moment out of time, never to be returned to, never repeated. She had acted inappropriately, she said, wrongly, and she hoped her mistakes could be forgiven. I nodded, thinking there had been no mistakes, no wrong, and nothing to forgive. Mrs. Jansen smiled and her smile was the saddest thing I had ever seen.

"And," she said. "There's something else I'm sorry for. You said something to me that afternoon, something very beautiful. It was a gift, and I was dismissive. But I want you to know that I did hear you, and I know. I accept your gift."

From down the hallway, I could hear a squeaky door and footsteps coming our way.

"I accept it," she said. "But I suspect it was really meant for someone else."

She handed me a copy of the textbook and told me to open it, quickly.

"The someone else," she said, quietly, quickly, "you might not believe in her, but she's there. She's in the world right now, and waiting for you."

Glancing at the page I had opened to, she said, more loudly as the footsteps approached, "By the end of the story, Nick has undergone a kind of healing, see? He has come through the burned-over landscape and gone into the river and he has had success with his fishing. You know by the end that even though he might not be completely okay yet, he's going to be. Oh, hi, honey."

The fireman stood in the doorway in his blue uniform, taut and observant, as if he watched for errant sparks. He seemed now almost to be sniffing for the first faint trace of smoke.

"Thought I was picking you up out front," he said.

Mrs. Jansen checked her watch and said she had thought she had ten more minutes. She'd been helping a student, nodding at me. The fireman nodded in turn. Mrs. Jansen said we'd have to finish up another time, she had to leave for an appointment with her husband, but I understood the story now, didn't I? I understood what she had been explaining? I did. I hoisted my backpack onto one shoulder. The fireman kept his place in the doorway and stared at me.

"At the bonfire," I said. "When Fats, I mean Warren, was up on the roof? And you kept him from jumping? That was." I stuck my hand out. "That was great. I just wanted to say."

The fireman's grip was crushing. "Just my job." He was looking past me at his wife. "We all just do our jobs."

The P.C. Office Supply Christmas party had once been a family affair, complete with Santa—the now-retired warehouse manager, Pat, whose red nose nicely finished off the rented costume—handing out presents to employees' children. But, these days, with no young kids to treat and with everything that was going wrong thanks to that hapless sonofabitch in the White House, the party was mostly bourbon and beer under a tattered "Merry Christmas" banner and a sprig of plastic mistletoe bought at the drugstore by the Secretary of Christmas Past. By the time my mother and I arrived, it was well underway, the Ray Coniff singers ruining "Good King Wenceslas" through tinny speakers, no one paying attention amidst the tipsy chatter. Married salesmen gathered in knots with their wives while the younger warehouse guys tried to figure out how to sneak a young woman under the fake mistletoe.

There was no sign of my father.

I hadn't known we were going to the party, hadn't known, even, that this was the night of the party, until, an hour earlier, my mother had come into my room and told me to get ready, we were going to meet my father at the office. My best shirt was the one with green stripes and squiggles, but it had been in the laundry and smelled. My mother had said it didn't matter, we wouldn't be staying at the party long and I could freshen it up with a Bounce sheet and five minutes in the dryer. When I was ready, she handed me a Tupperware of oatmeal cookies.

"They aren't Christmas cookies," she said, "but they're the only kind we had the ingredients for."

There were no lights on at Nicole's as we passed, no cars at the curb. The house had seemed deserted for a week or more. "Tie a Yellow Ribbon" was on the radio again as we passed, but they were playing that song a lot these days and in the yards along Centertown Road people had really tied yellow ribbons on trees. My mother switched to the station that played carols 24/7 starting the day after Thanksgiving.

We stood in the office doorway for a minute until Mr. Clifford noticed us and came over, saying *Merry Christmas* through his stretched grin and kissing my mother on the cheek. He shook my hand and said he was happy to see us, he hadn't known we were coming.

"We misplaced the invitation, somehow," Will's mother said. She had only realized when Cheryl, Mrs. Clifford, called to ask which kind of cookies she was going to bring, and Clifford said why didn't I go on and take those cookies over to the refreshments table. His wife was over there and she could help me find a plate to put them on. He wrinkled his nose and I could smell the hamper mildew odor rising from my shirt. I could get myself some punch over there too, Clifford said. As I walked away, I heard Clifford explain that my father had had to run out at the last minute to see a client but that he'd be back any minute. This was the kind of dedication that made him such an asset to the company.

The table was decorated with fold-out tissue-paper bells of green and red and someone had scattered glittery stars over the white paper tablecloth. Plates of cookies sat between big bowls of potato chips and in the middle a punchbowl held a couple of gallons of the Hawaiian Punch and Ginger Ale concoction. It was hard to see why so much of it was needed here. All the grownups were drinking booze, even Clifford, as he stepped into his office to make a phone call. Cheryl Clifford hugged me and said, "Merry Christmas! You've gotten so tall, everybody's getting so big now and changing so much and bless my heart what lovely cookies." She took the Tupperware and set the cookies out on a Santa-shaped platter. They looked brown and plain alongside the frosted sugar Christmas trees. I ladeled some punch into a cup and watched Clifford talking urgently into his phone. When Clifford hung up, he beckoned me into his office.

"It's good to see you and your momma," he said. "How are y'all doing?"

"We're fine," I said. "But I think my mom expected to see my dad here."

"Well," Clifford said. "I know he'll be glad to see y'all here when he gets back from this emergency thing with a client. He hated to run off during the party, you know."

When I did not reply, he set his glass down on the desk and shut the door.

"All right, son," he said. "I won't bullshit you. He's having a rough time, your old man."

"A rough time, sir?"

"Comes a time for most men," Clifford said, perching on the corner of his desk and looking not at me but into some immeasurable distance above and beyond my head, "when every dish loses its savor. When he realizes that the plain fact of the matter is that he's not done what he once thought he might do, hasn't become what during his best and most hopeful youthful moments he had ambitions to become. Comes a time, and that time is different for each man, but for most men that time will come, will come for you, too, though you're too young for it yet, when those things that he once prized, those things that gave him pleasure or excitement, whether the scotch whiskey," he swirled the brown liquid in his glass, "or the woodworking, the sports car or even the fine-skinned breast of a woman, are as so much ash upon the tongue. *The world is vanity and the people of the world is grass.*" Clifford smoothly drank the inch of whiskey and poured another from the bottle.

"Now," he said, "the preachers will counsel prayer and works, and the head-shrinkers will call it adjustment disorder and recommend exercise, and you see plenty of men who have arrived at this point walking their miles around the piped ponds of city parks. *Be with people,* they'll say. *Go in together for that group appetizer deal at Chili's and remember how to laugh.* But what they fail to say, fail to see, maybe, I don't know, but what they leave out, anyway, is that what that man is at that moment having trouble adjusting to is nothing more or less than the bitter pith of meaninglessness, the hollow at the heart, his own heart and the heart of the universe. Comes a time like that for a man, and some manage it through the stubborn persistence of the basest appetites. Never in all my years of hunting deer did I shoot so many and so well as during that spell when my soul had dried to a husk, and one chilly afternoon outside of Iredell, son, I shoved my hand into the hot chest of a dying doe and carved her beating heart out and I about wore my jaw to wreckage working my teeth through its toughness because if I was going to live I was going eat life even if it tasted like pennies and burnt hair. A man can get to the other side of those leaden moments, even when those moments last for years. But some don't. Some succumb. And your old man, young William. Well, I can't say." He shook his head. "I just can't say."

It took me a minute to figure out that that was all, that the conversation was over. I thanked Mr. Clifford and left his office. The tinny carols were like foil against my teeth, and I didn't want to run into my mother, so I refilled my cup with punch and headed for the welcoming darkness of the warehouse. I knew the way through the broad concrete aisles. I avoided the pallet jacks and forklifts parked along one wall and followed the shelving, turning twice, feeling the cases of paper and ink towering over me. The smells changed as I moved through cleaning fluids and six sizes of Rubbermaid wastebaskets. The light in the little warehouse office was on and in the illuminated window I saw my father buckling his pants and straightening his tie. I stepped back into the shadows and watched my father lead a woman I did not recognize out of the little cubby, locking the door behind them and hurrying toward the loading dock at the back of the building. Suddenly, all I could smell was the stink of my shirt, damp rot under the dryer sheet's perfume.

To step from the warehouse back into the office was to step from a dusky church onto a sunlit thoroughfare. Voices buzzed and laughter honked here and there, the tinny carols jingling around it all. My mother stood with some of the wives, far from the punchbowl. One of the women was talking and laughing, the others smiling along, my mother nodding and sipping from her cup but not smiling as she kept looking toward the door. Six of the twelve days of Christmas had passed with their gifts before my father entered the party, back from his client call, grinning to colleagues and kissing the cheeks of their wives as he moved through the knots of drinkers toward my mother.

I was too far away, the carols too loud, for me to hear the words that passed between my parents, but the pantomime was legible, my smiling father's move to kiss his wife prevented by her hand upon his chest, the impact of her words forcing him back a step and rearranging the features of his face. They stood a few feet apart, tense and silent, before my father's face reassumed its salesman's smile. It was Christmas time, he had been working hard, and he didn't understand why she was so upset, why they had to go right then, what she was talking about because he had indeed been meeting with a client, as anyone there would tell her, and the reason his car had been in the parking lot was easy to explain. It had been running rough, certainly she had heard that, and he'd be taking it to the shop over the weekend but in the meantime he'd need to make this quick run to Irving and so he had borrowed Pasco's car, *just ask Pasco for Christ's sake*, but she didn't need to ask Pasco or anyone else because a woman knew, she just knew. Finally, his shoulders shrugged and his hands spread to take in the whole grimly festive space, until my mother spoke again and turned, her eyes tearing and skimming the room for a sign of her son. "Come on," she said when she got to me through the parting audience, and when I said we had just gotten there she reminded me that she'd said we would not be staying long.

"What's going on?"

"You can ask your father when he gets home," she said. "If he gets home."

My father, it turned out, would not be coming with us. Having just arrived at the party—or, as my mother said, yanking the gearshift down and stomping on the gas so that the tires spun and spat pebbles, having just re-arrived at the front part of the party—that man was planning to stay for a while.

Later, I lay awake. I had not out-walked even the nearest streetlight. My mother had gone straight to bed, reminding me that there was leftover Sloppy Joe in the refrigerator. It was too cold for a long walk and halfway down the block, knowing without having to see that there were no lights on at Nicole's house, I had given up and committed myself to the penitential confines of my own room, lying for hours now, it seemed, listening to the speakers hiss and hum after the last record had stopped spinning and the needle's arm had settled into its cradle. Phrases resounded in the dark until, finally, headlights carved a momentary path along the wall. Tires and engine followed, slowed, stopped, and after the car door chunked shut unsteady footsteps marched, keys jangled and finally found the lock. My father made no effort to be quiet. The door's slam was like a shot, and I could not tell who shouted first. My mother seemed to shoot into the living room to meet my father as he limped out of the hall and immediately they compared embarrassments and, finding no clear victor there, rose or descended through the familiar curses and quickly reached the argument over which of them should leave and how and whether the one who left should ever even *think* of coming back because, guess what, you never knew what you might find and one or the other by the time the one who left returned might have a whole new life and whatever that life was it would be an improvement on the present one that was for goddamn sure.

The pillow I held over my ears did not help much but it was, like the closed door of my room, a layer of something at least between me and the storm that moved from room to room and finally down the short hall with my father's approaching shout that if he was going to be thrown out of his own house he was damn well going to have Christmas with his son first, all protection falling away as the door slammed open and the overhead light blazed on. My father tossed a package, wrapped in metallic green paper, onto my bed while my mother screeched at me, "Leave that there and do not open it," and, at my father, "How dare you bring family Christmas into this? Where was all this worry about family this afternoon?"

"Merry goddamn Christmas," my father said. "Open your goddamn present."

I left the package where it lay and wished that I had not undressed for bed, that I was wearing something more than shorts and a threadbare T-shirt. I might as well be naked.

"Fine, then," my father snorted, turning and stalking back down the hall. I quickly slipped back into jeans and my Payne Track and Field sweatshirt. Neither parent was in the living room when I emerged, nor was anyone in the kitchen. I could hear one parent loudly opening dresser drawers and yanking hangers full of clothes from the closet in their bedroom. A suitcase was flung onto the floor. The angel-decorated clock over the fireplace ticked and a flaming sword swung over the gate.

In the bathroom, though I tried not to look, the way I always tried not to look because if you're careful you can go through whole days of not seeing yourself and those days allow you to forget, to imagine someone who looks unlike you, someone who doesn't really look like anything, moving through the world unlooked at, someone unremarkable moving around unremarked, I caught a glimpse of my face in the mirror. There were people who lived all the time without having to worry about being seen, people who, by some occult combination of luck and design, might as well have been invisible. I could believe myself, sometimes, for an hour, for a day if I was careful, to be one of these, could run along the street or around the track, could ride across town, unseen or if seen unnoticed or if noticed left alone. And then you walked by the bathroom mirror, dimly illuminated by the nightlight you hadn't really needed since third grade, and, distracted by the thumping and grumbling from another room, you let your glance slide just that little bit and saw there, staring back at you, that feral, fearful face with which you had to face the faces that you faced.

How the storm that had been thundering along in my parents' bedroom exploded out onto the front yard I could not say. A shriek had shattered the face in the mirror and we were all suddenly, in the jagged transitionlessness of a dream, standing outside, my mother laughingly holding up my father's keys, my father snorting and hoofing at the grass, and me planted like an ornament under the porch light and seeing, one after another, lights come on in windows up and down the street. So he wanted to go, my mother was shouting, then it must be because he was going to go to wherever that bitch was, whoever that bitch was.

"That's right, b-i-t-c-h, bitch bitch bitch!" And she was damned if he was going to drive away to that bitch, he could walk. "Oh you're the bitch," my father was shouting. "Bitch bitch bitch is all you do is all you are and you're goddamn right I'm going because even though I left everything I wanted to do and be just to take care of you and because," looking at me, "you couldn't take care of *him*, you're throwing me out of my own goddamned house."

"Then walk," my mother shouted.

"Give me the keys," my father shouted.

And when my mother reared back and threw the keys, I thought my father and I were equally surprised at how high and how far they flew, at how they jingled and twinkled against the streetlight and then disappeared into the dark. And when my father stormed across the lawn I thought my mother and I were equally surprised at how quickly he moved, bad toes and all, and how loud the crack was when his fist connected with her jaw and how suddenly she was not a woman standing and screaming but was instead a body slumped against the front passenger side tire. And when I did not move, when I was frozen to the spot there under the porch light, I thought the neighbors and I must be equally surprised at the way this athletic teenager stood impotently by and did nothing, nothing at all, not even when the ambulance at last arrived.

20.

I ALMOST DIDN'T HEAR NICOLE when she knocked on my window. This was not because I was asleep. I wasn't sleeping much, and when I did manage to drop off I'd dream about that night again, my father charging across the yard, my mother's jaw breaking under his fist with a crunching sound that grew, in every iteration, louder and more shattering, my own feet stuck in the nightmarish muck of the yard, unable to move, my throat frozen, the words of defense or prevention stuck like sharp and splintered bones there. It was Tom Petty who almost made me miss her that night, maybe a week after my parents' fight, telling me in my headphones that I didn't have to live like a refugee. I don't know how long she'd been standing out there, knocking quietly on my window, but as the song ended I heard a noise that wasn't the hiss of the needle in its groove or the thump of it knocking every second or so in the little scratch on the record.

Was I surprised to see her out there? I'm not sure what could have surprised me more. There she was, though, her hair pulled back and hidden under a stocking cap, her inadequate plastic jacket zipped against the cold. I wanted to let the curtain swing back into place and hide her, to let her knock until she tired of it and went away. I wanted to tell her to fuck off with Heidi D'Amico, to ride alongside as Heidi drove too fast and missed a curve and flew her Sunbird off the road and into a tree or over a cliff or anywhere that was far from me. I opened the window.

"What are you doing here?" I whispered.

"We need to talk."

"But I'm a creep, remember? I'm supposed to stay away from you."

"Heidi can be a bitch," she said. "Are you going to come out?"

When I met her at the front door, I handed her the coat I had taken from the coat rack in the hall. It was a heavy one my father wore when he had to go with Paschal or Clifford on a hunting trip.

"Here," I said. "That jacket you're wearing is useless."

She shrugged into the coat. It was way too big for her and in it she looked tiny, fragile. How could someone who looked like this be so intimidating, so cruel?

"Come to the park," she said.

"My aunt and uncle are staying here," I said. "To take care of my mom. I'm not supposed to leave the house."

"I heard about your mom," she said. "That sucks."

In the cold, her face seemed taut even without its usual makeup mask. Her nose shone a little in the streetlight's pale illumination and her eyes gleamed.

"But were you allowed to go riding around town at night before?"

"What do you want, Nicole?"

"I want to tell you something, okay? Jesus. Come to the park."

There was no moon that night, and once we had made our way through the shadows of the cottonwood, we emerged not into a magically transformed playground but, instead, into a general darkness in which loomed, here and there, deeper darknesses. The grass, shorn for the coming winter and now starting to grow a coat of frost, crunched underfoot. Nicole stumbled on something neither of us saw, but I did not offer her my hand. She caught herself and walked on, hands jammed into the pockets of my father's coat, until we got to the swings.

"Okay," I said. "We're here. What did you want to tell me."

She sat in one of the swings, hands still in the coat pockets. The chain creaked and scraped.

"I don't owe you an apology," she said.

"You had to drag me to the park in the middle of the night to tell me that?"

She dug her feet into the ditch that had been worn under the swing and twisted away from me, then let the straightening of the chains carry her back.

"I owe you an explanation," she said.

She unzipped my father's coat and dug around with her hand. I couldn't see what she was doing until she flicked the lighter into life.

"Do you mind?" she said around the cigarette she had put between her lips.

"Whatever," I said.

"You're sweet," she said, when she had blown a stream of smoke away from me. "You're sweet and you were sweet to me and you deserve better. But."

"Yeah," I said. "But."

But, she continued, things were fucked up. In some other world, maybe there would be a chance for something between us, because she liked me and she knew that I liked her. But, again, things were fucked up. I wanted to say just how deeply I realized things were fucked up, what with my mom in the hospital and my old man holed up in the motel after his one night in jail, but something was stuck in my throat and I couldn't talk. What fucked things up, she said, was that she hung out with Hector's friends and in the world they made, something like us never had a chance.

"Whatever it was," she said, "you watching me and me knowing you were there and that night when we rode your bike and kissed, it was a nighttime thing."

"Yeah," I managed to croak out.

She smoked for a minute and then said that the problem was that it was not the only nighttime thing, as I knew. There was Hector. And it might have been possible to see me and keep it from Hector, to never let him think that anybody knew, and that was what she had been thinking, as much as she was thinking at all, that was what she was figuring might just be possible, but then I had gotten myself onto Hector's radar.

"That night, the night before Thanksgiving, when you came to my house," she said. "Heidi and I were going to this party and Hector wasn't going to go, but then when you gave him that card with the note to me, he decided to show up. He didn't go with us. He came later. It wasn't that he thought you were going to be there. He wasn't showing up to beat you up or something. You're the kind of person who's invisible to him, and this was a party with a lot of his friends, not a place where someone like you was going to be. And it was chill, at first, the kind of thing Heidi and I spend a lot of time at, like when Hector and his friends race their cars in the Bottoms and everybody stands around drinking beer and smoking and someone's radio is blaring. This was the usual kind of party, just loud music and drinking and smoking, some people pairing off and going to the bedrooms of this kid's house up in Woodbriar. His parents were away for the holiday weekend and they'd left him there."

I had ridden my bike through the curving lanes and cul-de-sacs of Woodbriar, one of the newer, nicer developments on the north side of town. The yards were big and boasted big trees even though the houses were only a few years old. Most of the houses had swimming pools out back, and it was easy to imagine the party she described. I'd seen things like it on TV.

"You know," she said. "I talked about you with Heidi." She sipped smoke and blew it out with a hiss. "Or I tried to. She didn't let me say a lot. You're not the kind of person who's really visible to her either. I didn't tell her about you seeing me, I couldn't, she doesn't really know about Hector. About what he does. And I didn't tell her about riding around on your bike that night. That was, I don't know, like, just for me. Not that I wanted to hide it, not the way you think. It was just mine. It was precious, kind of, like nothing else that had ever happened to me. It was like a jewel. I wrapped it up in velvet and kept it safe because it wouldn't be safe with Heidi. She'd laugh at it and shit on it."

"It was precious to me, too," I whispered.

"Anyway," she went on, "so it's late and everybody's drunk and stoned and some of the pairs that had paired off had left and some of the people who hadn't paired off were doing that kind of predator-prey thing you see late at night, and I saw Hector talking to this friend of his, Ronnie, I don't know if you know this guy at all, he was a couple of years ahead of me and I'm ahead of you so he left school before you started at Payne. He works at the pizza place by the highway ramp. But they were looking at me and talking and then Hector came over to where I was with Heidi, we were sitting out on this little patio and smoking and looking at the stars, she's really into astrology and she was telling me again about zodiac symbols and what they mean and all, and Hector comes over and pulls me away and says I've got to go to one of the bedrooms with this guy, Ronnie, this friend of his, because he just sold me to him."

"Sold you?"

Hector, it turned out, always needed money. The muffler shop paid, what, twice minimum wage or something, decent but not enough to support the Camaro and the girls and some of his other habits. Dealing paid him some, but he would get into cash-flow trouble there. This guy, Ronnie, had had a thing for Nicole for a long time. She had known. Caught him watching when a bunch of them were hanging out. She didn't know whose idea it was. Probably Hector's.

"But you can imagine, right," she said. "Ronnie says wow, he'd pay to fuck me and he's probably joking, mostly, but he kind of means it too, and my brother takes him seriously and says *yeah, I could make that happen.* Anyway, it was presented to me as a done deal. Hector was getting three hundred and Ronnie got to fuck me in one of the bedrooms. Heidi told him off, said there was no way he could pimp me out like that, but he told her to shut up, it wasn't like I was a virgin, he could probably have gotten five if I'd been a virgin. I didn't say anything. Heidi could storm all she wanted, she didn't have to go home with him, be home with him. Share home with him. And she doesn't know about how he is, you know, what he does to me. If I fought with him, it would all just be worse. I'd still end up getting fucked by Ronnie but then there would be Hector to deal with, too. And Ronnie's sweet, I like him okay. Not like I would have chosen to sleep with him, but he's okay. Part of me was like, y*eah, like Hector said, I'm no virgin*."

She took a deep drag from the cigarette and flicked the butt away. I followed the glow and walked over and crushed it with my foot.

"Look," she said. "I haven't been with a ton of guys, okay. But I've slept with a couple, okay? And I've done other things, you know, let them do other things. I'm not confused about sex and love, right? It's like weed, you know? I like the way I feel when I get high but I don't think the pot's in love with me."

We both stood in the quiet for a minute and let the chilly breeze and rattle of frozen leaves and the click of bare branches in the trees and the cold creak of the swing chain say what we both knew: that I was in love with her.

"But always before that," she said, "even if I didn't feel like I loved the guy, at least I had picked him. Not the very first time, that was a whole other kind of fucked up, this other friend of Hector's, surprise surprise, who didn't know the meaning of no. At least he pulled out at the last second. And not the stuff with Hector, of course, but all he ever does is feel me up. The thing was, I haven't made out with anybody that I didn't, in some way, choose to make out with. And here's something you should know. I had chosen not to make out with anybody since that night with you. But then here I was, being led by Ronnie to the back bedroom and everybody who was still at the party, everybody who was still conscious, anyway, was watching us leave the living room. They all knew we were going to fuck in that back bedroom, and it felt like they knew that it was all Hector's doing, and I felt like I was naked already, naked in front of them all, like my clothes had been ripped off of me, like my skin, even, had been peeled off and they were seeing not just me in this tight top and jeans but me flayed open and I could feel their eyes on my nerves because this was when everyone would know that Nicole Rose was a slut pimped out by her brother. And the whole time he was kissing me and peeling off my top and pushing up inside me I was just like *no, I did not choose this*, Hector did, and he did it for three hundred, but more than that he did it to show me that he could, that it didn't matter who I wanted to be with because I had to be with whoever *he* said."

Nicole's voice had stayed even throughout. If not for the way my eyes had naturally adjusted to the darkness so that, as she spoke, I could see her face ever more clearly, I would not have known how it hurt for her to remember and to tell. But tears had gathered in the telling and they had dripped without a fuss down both of her cheeks as she spoke.

"And then you ran into me the next day."

"Heidi couldn't take anything out on Hector," she said. "Not in any way that mattered. So you were convenient."

I was sorry. That I had delivered that stupid card, that I might have encouraged Hector to flex his muscles, that this thing had happened to her. It was okay, she said, she was okay. Ronnie had been sweet, not rough like Hector was. She shivered, and I could not know whether it was from the cold or for some other reason.

"You know that movie, *The Empire Strikes Back*?"

"The *Star Wars* movie?"

Whoever it was that usually slept in the back bedroom where she had gone with Ronnie, someone's little brother who was conveniently away that week, that kid had an *Empire Strikes Back* poster on his wall, one with Luke Skywalker and the what was he called, wockie or whatever, the big hairy thing. Nicole said she had stared at the poster the whole time this Ronnie guy was on top of her, slobbering on her neck and pumping between her legs, stared at the black mask of Darth Vader in the background and the sandy blonde surfer-looking hero and his oversized dog wearing bandoleros. She saw that picture now when she closed her eyes. It hadn't been so bad, really, Ronnie had been sweet to her, but that poster hung in her mind like a black cloud no wind could blow away.

"One thing I can tell you," she said. "I am never going to watch that stupid fucking movie."

I stepped closer to her, close enough that she could lean into my chest and I could put my arms around her. We stayed that way for a while, Nicole's face pressed against my jacket, and that was good because she could not then see any of the things that were happening in my face, the wobble of my chin as I fought tears of impotent and anguished rage.

"God," I finally whispered. "God, I hate this fucking town."

She laughed. "You and me both, man."

I stepped back and lifted her chin with my hand so that I could look into her eyes.

"We could leave," I said. "Let's leave. Let's just go and leave it all behind us."

"Take this circus all the way to the border?" she said. She was smiling (at least I was pretty sure she was smiling), but her voice was already pulling away from me, sinking back into herself, leading or following as she began to take the steps that would carry her away from me forever.

"Yes," I said, almost shouted, as if more volume in my voice, more intensity in my saying this, would carry her along. "Really. I mean it. If we gathered up whatever money we can get and some clothes and stuff. We could take my mother's car. We could be far enough by morning that no one could find us."

She stood up from the swing and kissed me. It was not a kiss that said we were going anywhere. When her tongue brushed my lips, I tasted the bitter smoke that lingered in her mouth, and when I licked my lip as she drew away, it, too, tasted faintly of cold ash.

"You're so sweet," she said. "You are so sweet and things are so fucked up. I've got to go."

I asked if we would come here again, to the park, together. If she would meet me here, maybe not tomorrow or the next night but sometime. If I could come to call her from her bedroom or if she would come to invite me from mine. She waved without turning back to face me, walking back toward her own street, her own house, and I knew that I would have to walk alone back to mine. I knew what the answers to my questions were.

21.

PARENTS' WEEKEND IS HERE, the rooms cleaned and straightened for display, the lounge and library swept and re-ordered, the lawns raked, and only this last night before they come. He has so dreaded this weekend that he lets himself think, sometimes, that it is no more than his parents' imminent arrival that the angelic squirrel threatens to foretell, that all this foreboding condensed into the claws poised over what must be simply a natural flaw in the chest fur is the normal freshman's fear of losing those freedoms recently found, of returning to a role recently abandoned. Up and down the corridor, as dirty laundry is hidden and shelves are dusted, others must be feeling something similar. But when the squirrel arrives at its appointed hour, all such reassuring thoughts fly out to join the last falling leaves as the wind whips them into dancers and leaves them at last to collapse, the squirrel in the stillness standing on his desk, stuffing crumbs into its cheeks and waiting. It knows something, wants to show him something, and the something seems to him, though this might simply be because they will arrive tomorrow, about his parents, Parents' Weekend having loomed since he first got here like a thunderhead over the calendar. He can see them, the squirrel innocently chewing at oatmeal, cowed by the campus, by the way he, too, is unfamiliar, made strange by his sojourn in the fields of knowledge. They will sit, a seedy town restaurant table between them, and make awkward small talk over lunch. They will sit, it seems, in the offices of his professors, so Seymour has suggested, and hear of his progress, and it is this, the image of his parents invading this space he has made his own, this space in which he has been making a self all his own, that brings him, the squirrel grown finally complacent and sluggish on its fattening diet, to lunge across the desk—now, now!—and tackle the beast, taking it by the throat and lifting it, a sacrifice, thumbs pressing at its windpipe.

22.

THE PLAN WAS INGENIOUS, REALLY. Denied by Fats's crazy dance atop the gym wall at their Homecoming bonfire, the students of Payne and their families and the fans of the Pirates and those who just liked to come out for the autumn spectacle persuaded the school administration and the Centertown city council that a Christmas bonfire would be a nice consolation blaze. On the one hand, it was just bringing outdoors the Yule log tradition that had—somebody looked it up—been around for hundreds of years, and, on the other hand, well everybody really had been looking forward to the Homecoming bonfire and disappointed when that fat kid tried to kill himself. Denied their public burning, Reverend Alan and Mrs. Kramer first joined the supporters of the Christmas conflagration and then, quietly, reminded the parents who had brought their kids' Satanic records and backmasked messages, that since there was going to be a fire anyway and since those evil inflammables were still reeking of the paraffin in which they had been soaked back in September, they could bring that stuff along and, at the right moment, transform one fire into another. Word of this conspiracy had almost certainly gotten to the leaders of the town and school, but there was little interest there in preventing it. Why shouldn't some infernal merch be thrown in to burst out in righteous flame or melt into toxic sludge? And just to be sure there were no causes for sudden cancellation or public concern, an extra tank truck would be borrowed from Arlington and all access to school buildings, inside or out, would be blocked off for the occasion.

I knew about the plans, but I was not paying them much attention. My father had spent only the one night in jail, but he was living, for the moment, in the motel out near his office. The hospital had released my mother after a couple of days, her broken jaw wired so that she could speak only through gritted teeth and had to take all of her meals through straws. Sue and Earl were caring for my mother, filling the blender with frozen berries and ice cream, grinding the pain pills so they could be mixed into milkshakes. With little else to do, Earl tinkered around the house, making little repairs that had gone unaddressed for a while and—when the towel racks had been tightened, the leaky faucet fixed, the holes in walls patched and re-painted, the loose edge of a carpet tacked back down—inventing new jobs that needed to be done. Any time I was home, I got drafted into these, made to hold a board while Earl sawed, to hold a handful of nails while Earl drove them.

To avoid my mother's tears and my uncle's urge to order, I stayed away from home. On wet afternoons, I walked to the Centertown library and read, or pretended to read, wandering the stacks until I had half a dozen volumes and then sitting in a corner of the reading room until closing time. If the day was just chilly, I crossed the athletic fields and hid out in the thicket, paging through the fat English book until some passage caught my eye. I had been curious about the story Mrs. Jansen mentioned when her husband showed up at the classroom, something about a guy fishing for trout, it sounded like a story I might like, but I could not find it in the book. I figured I would ask Mrs. Jansen about it if I could ever find a chance. She was hard to talk to these days, busy after class and leaving school as soon as the last bell rang. Sometimes Bo was waiting for her and she climbed into the pickup truck with him. A couple of times, though, I had watched from the edge of the woods as she had driven her Celica out of the school parking lot and, after a quick walk to the edge of the ravine, I had seen through the screen of leafless trees her gray car crawl along the back of the clinic lot and park beside the dumpster, out of sight of the street.

The day before the bonfire, pickup trucks had dropped loads of wood—logs the size of telephone poles and pallets stacked with shorter lengths—and on the day of the fire groups of students and adults had built the pyre. By the time I left the building that afternoon, the chaotic pile had mostly been transformed into an orderly progression of platforms that rose like the stories of a building, each a little smaller than the one beneath, and culminated in a spire of slanted, overlapping two-by-fours. Walking by it, I could smell the gas-soaked rags that had been stuffed into the lumber here and there. When they lit it that night, the wood was going to burn like hell.

I had never seen Fats Crandall in a baseball cap before, but there he was with a group of others in similar caps, helping to pick up unused scraps of wood and pile them into a wheelbarrow. The front of the cap bore a big white cross and said "Saved." I recognized some of the other kids from the Reverend Alan's group.

"Warren?"

Fats tossed splintery scraps into the wheelbarrow.

"Hi, William," he said. It was good to see me, he said. He had meant to come and find me sometime because he needed to talk to me. A girl named Kasey—Kasey with a K—came over and reminded Fats that they were going to pick up pizzas and then go back to the church for fellowship when they were done and was he coming because if so he could ride with them. She smiled at me and said there was always room for one more. When she had gone back to the woodpile, I asked if Fats had joined up with the twice-born.

"They're nice," Fats said. They were the nicest people he had ever known. Reverend Alan had come by the hospital after Fats had tried to jump. At first, Fats had not wanted him there, had said nothing when the minister spoke to him, one finger always stuck between the pages of the floppy black Bible, had refused to bow his head or let the minister take his hand while he prayed. But after a couple of visits, things that minister said started to make a lot of sense. Like Jesus was a social outsider, nobody liked him either and look what they had finally done to him. And who had he loved the most, who had he said would join him in his kingdom? Well, the other social outsiders, of course, and when they had, when they had just said to him, even in the quietest little voice, that they were broken and sinful and they needed the Lord, when they opened up their heart to him just that little bit, well then Jesus came all the way into them and they were from that moment saved from the pain of loneliness and insult, saved in a way that made the cowardly escape of jumping from the gym roof look just like the Devil's invitation that it was, because, though Fats might not know this, the Devil had sure enough said to Jesus that maybe he should jump from a high place too, and wouldn't Fats rather accept the invitation to be loved and saved than the one to jump and go splat on the asphalt and, afterwards, burn forever in the lake of fire?

Besides, they always went for pizza afterward.

"But these are the people who wanted kids to burn their records," I said. "To burn their clothes."

Fats stared at me as if I were a stranger and maybe by this time I was, so far now from the stockpile of snack cakes, from hobbits and nude models secreted in the foot locker.

"Now, " he said, "that stuff was already burning, don't you know?"

Why had things always been the way they were, why had he, Fats, always been picked on, why did he, Warren, have to be fat in the first place? But Reverend Alan had helped him to see. This was what happened with God, He showed you His love by showing you where your sinful habits led, and here Fats had been all his life, wanting nothing but to eat (gluttony) and fuck a girl (lust), reading nothing but books about worlds that didn't exist (that was some sin too, but he couldn't remember which), and God was saying, *well, if you eat all those burgers and ice cream, guess what, you're going be a fat fuck, and if you beat off about all those girls, you're going to make yourself disgusting to them, and if you lose yourself in fantasies you're going to make yourself unfit for the world you really live in.* That sounded like a shitty excuse for love to me, but Fats said it was the best love because it made you change and get better, or it could if you saw it for what it was.

"Sounds like my old man," I said. "This is for your own good. This hurts me as much as it hurts you."

Fats said He died, he said God became Jesus and died. If somebody could do that for you, then they really did love you, they had to, and the least he could do was accept that love and turn away from his own sick sinfulness.

"Look," he said, and pointed to the pyre. The first gas-soaked rag he had stuffed into a crack between some logs was his own Black Sabbath T-shirt. And it wasn't too late for me, either. Maybe all that had been going so badly for me was God's love too, it must be, and if I accepted it and saw my depravity for what it was then I could turn around and take God into myself and I could be saved too.

"Would I get a hat?" I said, and Fats said he would pray for me, then he turned and went to join the girl named Kasey-with-a-K.

23.

I ALMOST DIDN'T NOTICE THE RED FERRARI where it idled in the parking lot as I watched my former friend waddle away to his salvation, seeing, only when I turned to go, the red smudge against the leaden sky, the dark dropping earlier now, seeming to come even before the sun began to set.

"No sprints today?" Stark called as his window lowered.

"No sir," I said. It was a cross-training day and I had spent the hour before school lifting weights.

"Well, good luck with that training program," the doctor said, but what we both knew damn well was that it came down to whether you could gut it out in the stretch, because if you really wanted it, that was where it had to show. The doctor got out of his car and stretched. His pants did seem nice, and I wished I had a jacket like the doctor's, one with leather sleeves and a wool body, as if someone had taken an old-fashioned varsity letter jacket and made it respectable for a grownup. It cost, the doctor told me, a couple hundred bucks but it was worth it. "Check out the vintage Cowboys design." By the way, he wondered, had I ever been to Mexico. The doctor was thinking of heading down that way. There were, he knew, pyramids and jungles, places you could disappear into. There were beaches where you could sit and look out at a crystalline blue ocean and dig your feet into the warm sand and somebody would bring you drinks, nice cold ones with lime in them served in tall glasses full of ice.

"Imagine," the doctor said, "watching some beauty in a bikini sun herself on that beach all afternoon and then walking with her hand in hand to some little cabana. Oh the things you could do to a body like that, the things a body like that could do to you."

I knew that the doctor knew we were both picturing the same body.

"How's that sound, kid? How's that sound?"

"Perfect," I said.

"Perfect," the doctor said. "I thought so too."

And when there was a perfect thing you wanted, you knew what you had to do. It was just like a race. You put everything into it, you coordinated all your actions so no energy was wasted, and you drove straight on through the obstacles and toward that goal. Stark's eyes left my face, and I turned to see Mrs. Jansen walking toward us. She held her tight gray blazer closed against the chill, the lacy front of her blouse a wave of Cancun sea foam cresting over its lapels.

"Did you two see that bonfire they're building?"

She wouldn't be surprised, she went on, if they ended up burning down the whole school. What was it with this town and these big fires?

"Witches," Stark said. "You better be careful."

"They didn't burn witches so much," I said. "That was a myth. At least in America. Even in Europe, though, it was heretics they burned more than witches. Witches they hanged."

"Thanks for the history lesson," Stark said. "It's a comfort to know the future of Centertown is in such knowledgeable hands. And where," he turned to Mrs. Jansen, "is your stuff?" Something crackled in the air between them.

"Are you coming to the bonfire?" I said, to break the tension. Stark said no way and at the same time Mrs. Jansen said she might, with Bo, the static stiffening. She said she needed to talk to Dr. Stark, that she would see me soon, and as I walked away I heard her say to the doctor that she couldn't, she knew she had said before that she could, but she just couldn't. The doctor said they should just get in the car right now, it didn't matter about her stuff, and Mrs. Jansen said she would get in the car, but only to talk, they needed to talk, but she wasn't going to go.

24.

TURNS OUT, IT'S HARDER TO STRANGLE A SQUIRREL than he ever would have thought. He expected some difficulty in catching the creature, but that part went smoothly, all things considered. For all of its blackly gleaming sentience and threatening superiority, the thing is, after all, still just a squirrel, a squirrel's little brain capable only of a limited repertoire of responses. He's got his hands around its neck after just a quick scramble around the desk, no problem. No, the problems start then, because strangling takes some time and the little bastard has a powerful drive to keep on living. Something there is that it has not revealed, some part of its mission, they both know, remains incomplete and where he wants to keep it that way, the squirrel clearly needs to finish its job, to pull back the curtain, to reveal him as a creature driven and derided by delusion, but no, he won't see that, won't, though the sharp black claws scrabble at his forearms until they find purchase in his flesh and gouge a bloody channel. He's got his hands around the neck so that the buck teeth can't get him, and he shakes the trembling, scrambling body so that the claws come free and the back legs impotently bicycle. He squeezes the squirrel's airway shut as his own opens in a scream. It's a fighter, the squirrel, demonic, energetic, the black eyes gleaming with intention, promise, power, even as blood begins to seep around where they are bulging from their lids. He feels nothing in his forearms, though he can see, when he glances down, blood dripping from his bent elbow and puddling on the linoleum, garish against the dullness of the room, the cast-off catalogues and phone books, the battered particle board furniture, the pilled gray bathrobe hanging from its plastic hook. The squirrel struggles, a final spasm, and finally *falls limp in his hands, dead and defeated, a ragged bundle, now, of bristly dinge. It could, like any of its brethren, be one of the simply fallen, the little ignorable animal element of every autumn, though his heart still pounds at the sight of it.*

25.

I HAD JUST REACHED THE EDGE OF THE WOODS when I heard the squeal of tires and the gunning of an engine in the parking lot. The pickup was heading straight for the Ferrari, so fast it seemed that it would ram the red car or run right over it. At the last second, the driver braked. The truck's tires screamed against the pavement and the back end fishtailed. Mrs. Jansen opened the passenger side, the Ferrari between her and the truck, and tumbled out, not wearing the gray blazer now, her white blouse shimmering against the parking lot, the dead fields, and the stone surface of the school. Her husband stepped slowly from the truck, heroic Bo in his fireman's uniform, husband and wife facing each other across the hood of the Ferrari, the doctor stuck inside his car, the pickup right against his door, Mrs. Jansen's hands out to her sides. I was not able to hear what she was saying, whether she was saying anything, and suddenly her hands were up over her head, the way you do when you want to make something stop, and, at the same time, her husband raised his hand and pointed it at her. Mrs. Jansen definitely said something then, shaking her head, backing away, her voice rising, rising, breaking, the husband, his hand still pointing out in front of him, turning toward the car. I saw Bo's hand jump before I heard the shot and the shattering of the Ferrari's windshield and the choking scream of Mrs. Jansen, the shot nothing like shots sounded on TV. The teacher turned to run, but the fireman was not looking at her. He stepped right up to the driver's side window. Was Stark moving to get away, moving at all, speaking? Bo Jansen's hand jumped again and there were two more dull thuds.

Mrs. Jansen was running toward me, shouting at me to run, too, and I could see behind her the fireman turning from the red car and walking after his wife. I turned and ran into the safety of the trees. Mrs. Jansen would know where I was going, know to follow me. I could hide her in the thicket. We could hide together in the thicket. The pistol coughed. Sirens were approaching, wailing and looping. I scrambled into the hideaway and listened past the pounding of my heart, my breath ragged in my throat. The pistol coughed. The looping sirens came closer. The red and blue lights would be spinning and dying against the darkening sky as police cars screeched into the parking lot. The footsteps were heavy and irregular. I wanted to run out to meet them, but whose were they? I saw again the way the fireman's hand had jumped. The brush curtain parted and Mrs. Jansen stumbled into the thicket, the front of her blouse blooming red, roses on snow, she was coming to me now carrying roses against the snow-white of her blouse. The bouquet bloomed brightly against her white blouse, her breath whistling, the teacher moaning, the sirens ceasing even as the blue lights strobed through the naked trees. Once more the gun popped in the sudden silence.

26.

IT IS ONLY WHEN THE DOOR OPENS *and the knocking on it stops that he realizes that the pounding came not only from inside him, heart and head together hammering at ribs and skull, that the two muscular men who enter wearing matching shirts were at the door for some time. One shushes him now and only now does he feel the ragged mess the screams have left his throat. The dead squirrel lies on an unlit pyre of old phone books, his grimy pajamas are smeared with blood.*

Campus is gone for good, now. Something in the shaking of the squirrel has fixed the flickering but fixed it on the wrong side, stuck him in the alternate reality, the underworld of robed shades. He wakes in the infirmary, a bandage on one wrist, a name bracelet on the other, and out the window sees the ill-kept grounds, brown grass crisscrossed with paved walks along which stumble in their sweat pants and cardigans his fellows, the mad. Half-dragged, half-carried from his room and through the unit hallway last night, he took in the day room, the cigarette burned couch and card tables, the molded plastic chairs, in one of which Willoughby, chronic catatonic, sat and stared at nothing. He knows that he can't blame this vision on a sedative hangover. He has landed here, somehow, and, somehow, knows this is where he took off from as well. Campus is gone for good, the brick and stone and dark wood paneling, swept lawns and autumn leaves and leather-bound volumes, because campus never was.

27.

BY THE TIME THE POLICE CAME INTO THE THICKET, the whistling in Mrs. Jansen's breaths had stopped and she wasn't moaning anymore. A little blood leaked from the corner of her mouth. I wiped it away and kissed her, but then the blood was there again, there on her lips, on my mouth, tasting of pennies and lilies. It was okay, though, she would be okay. This I said to the policemen as they pulled the limbs and climbing brown brush away and shone their flashlights into the thicket. One spoke into the walkie-talkie whose squawking I had heard, had traced, as the cops made their way through the woods. The flashlight's beams hurt as they fell upon my eyes and another cop said to turn the light away from the kid's face for crying out loud. His voice was soft as he asked me if I was shot, if I was hurt or bleeding, soft as he said "Son we're here, we can take her now."

I would not let Mrs. Jansen go. She was resting, I said, Mrs. Jansen resting in my arms, quiet now, no whistling in her breath, no moans, and when the policemen had entered the thicket she had turned her face toward my chest. Everything was cold. Mrs. Jansen was cold, and my hands, and I could not stop shivering, but because she was in my arms she did not shiver. I would hold her, warm her. "Son, we can take her now, we can take her to the hospital, we can take you both, you can come with her."

I would not let Mrs. Jansen go, she was resting. In my arms, she did not shiver, and there was not even any blood now leaking from her mouth, as she rested her face against my chest, as she turned to me from the policemen who had entered with their flashlights and walkie-talkies the thicket, grot, hideout and haven, and who stood watching now as I held her, pennies and lilies in my mouth. "There's nothing to be afraid of now, son," the policeman said. "The man with the gun is dead, he killed himself. Nobody's going to do any more shooting. We are here to take her now, to take you both. We're taking you both to the hospital."

I would not let Mrs. Jansen go. Her arms were around me and I held her now as she had held me here in the thicket. I loved her now as she had loved me then, here, in the thicket, the cops' hands gentle as they lifted Mrs. Jansen's arm from around my waist where it had rested, where it could not stop my shivering though she had not shivered in my arms, gentle as they stopped her head from rolling as it did when the policeman took the weight of Mrs. Jansen's body from my lap where it had rested. Her face did not turn toward the policeman's chest as it had turned toward mine and the policeman's hand was gentle when I cried out that she wanted to stay with me, his voice gentle as he said that I could come too, that I should come, we would all go to the hospital together, the bouquet blooming bright and black in the flashlights' glare and Mrs. Jansen staring back at me, her eyes unmoving and unmoved, the man with the gun dead and no shooting anymore now. It was safe, the cop said, safe to leave this thicket, and I knew that he was lying, there was nowhere safe but here and here I would stay, pale and loitering. And then coming through the branches and the climbing brown brush that had been pulled back like curtains, my father tripped across the leaf carpet and fell on his knees and put his arms around me and said it was okay, it would be okay, and I was very glad to hear my father say this though I knew it was not true.

[184]

28.

BY THE TIME SEYMOUR COMES IN, *white blazered, bearing file folder and yellow pad, he has begun to absorb this, the way a fighter absorbs body blows, pain dulling to ache as bruises bloom and the deep tissues start to knit themselves anew. He hardly notices the tears that leak from the corners of his eyes and wend down his unshaved cheeks. This is not, Seymour says, how anyone had hoped for the breakthrough to come. The squirrel's body has been sent to the state lab for a rabies test, but it will come back negative, won't it, the animal had come into the room not because it was sick but because it had been trained to. It had gotten a good couple of gashes in as it struggled, but he did not lose too much blood, the claws had missed his arteries, and though he'd keep a scar as a memento there would be no lasting damage to the nerves or muscles. Seymour sits in the chair beside his bed. He has not noticed before the strands of gray that frame her face. She wonders, soft-voiced, what he can remember, not of last night and the squirrel, but from before.*

She came to him, he recalls. Came bearing roses that were not roses but blood, came from the place of fire in snow that was not snow. He had been running, always running, though he had been frozen, unable to run, until she came to him carrying blood, the fire built but not burning. Tears leak, unnoticed. She wonders, Seymour, does he know where he is. Beyond her, through the window, he can see the brown lawn and, crossing it on one of the diagonal paths, his mother and father. They walk alongside each other, not touching, not talking, each intent on the path, on the way to the infirmary where, someone has told them, they will find their son. His mother stumbles on a loose chunk of concrete and his father catches her arm, holds her up, holds her hand, then, as they contin-

ue. Yes, he remembers. When they brought him here, not to the infirmary last night but to the hospital last year, the year before, his father had said Willow Bend, eh, well I see the willow, scraggly thing there bowed over the pond, but what the hell's the bend? Yes, he remembers, his mother through her tears saying the bend is what they're going to fix here, maybe, what they're going to help him with. He nods, his mother now steering his father from the stubbing of a tortured toe, he remembers everything.